Bedtime S[illegible] for Kids and Toddlers

A COLLECTION OF MEDITATION TALES TO AVOID TEARS BEFORE BED AND HELP CHILDREN FALL ASLEEP FAST, HAVE BEAUTIFUL DREAMS, AND LEARN MINDFULNESS

SAMANTHA TRAVERS

TABLE OF CONTENTS

Daist

Introduction

Children often do not want to go to sleep, they say that's too soon, that they are not tired and parents are forced into a hard battle to convince them, sounds familiar?

The truth is , it's not easy to send children to sleep! Parents, almost always tired after a long day at work, have to face a real battle every night! They would really like their children to go to bed quietly, because they would like some time to relax after the hard day.

The refusal to go to sleep or sleep alone, the frequent awakenings at night actually hide other reasons that children do not know and express them.

The life that our children lead today is very hectic

and complex : a busy schedule at school , plus sports, hobbies, time spent playing with friends, many and many experiences that create in children a state of overexcitement difficult to "turn off". In addition to this, overexposure to technological devices heavily affects the ability to relax and sleep.

Moreover they think about something that happened to them during the day, something that gives them anxiety or stress, and they do not have the right tools to manage or control them.

It is therefore a good habit to make them listen to, or better yet tell, relaxing and sleep-inducing stories.

This book contains soothing tales with adventures of children, animals and fantastic characters; every story has a moral for children and teaches love for others, overcoming fears and anxieties, improving self-confidence, gratitude and acceptance.

In these stories you will find simple breathing and meditation exercises, made especially for children, which will bring their mind into a state of relaxation and tranquility, a prelude to a good quiet and deep sleep. These simple exercises are an integral part of the story and are presented as a game of participation in the story itself. The child is driven to imagine scenes, colors, animals and will feel more than spectator of the adventure.

These exercises are also useful to stimulate the ability of the visual and imagination of the mind of our children, capacity today too often mortified by the enormous amount of images to which we are all subjected.

This overexposure to the images that come from television, computers, tablets, billboards etc. do not stimulate but absorb the natural ability of visuality of the mind, because you no longer have to strive to "create the image", as it is already proposed beautiful and packaged!

Meditation, on the other hand, pushes the mind into an area of silence where it can express its real possibilities. With meditation and breathing techniques, the child learns to have more control over the reactions of his body, managing to overcome anxiety and stress and learning to stay more focused, which will be very useful even in everyday life and school commitments.

In many schools, teachers have introduced moments of meditation for the class, verifying that it has a very good result in terms of concentration and success for all schoolchildren, who benefit enormously.

So meditation, whose efficacy is now worldwide recognized, can be useful to calm down children mind accompanying them into a state of relax that can assure them a deep ,good, restorative sleep time, with no nightmares.

Little by little meditation will become a regular habit wich will also help them to grow up as more confident, focused, loving adults able to manage their emotions.

In the pre-sleep phase the brain is more receptive to receiving and storing information, so it is therefore a perfect time, through stories of experiences and adventures and our simple techniques of meditation, to understand emotions, love others, improve self-awareness and learn to control one's moods

These stories can be read in any order you like, so please do feel free to skip around and choose which stories you think your child will like best for each night.

The tone of the stories should be fun but also relaxing and help children create imaginative and stimulating images in their minds, in which they can recognize themselves or they can refer them to everyday experiences or even live fantastic adventures!

For parents listening with children, or even reading these stories, this is an especially important time of sharing and participating in their growth;

they become unforgettable moments for both parents and children.

... but remember: FIRST OF ALL TURN OFF ALL “BLU LIGHT” DEVICES ... your mind will thank you, and also the mind of your children!

Chapter 1

Overcome Fear, Shyness and Anger

THE OWL AND THE OPEN WINDOW

The time has come to call it a night.

The sun has set and the lights in all the homes are warm and glowing.

When the sun goes down, we are all preparing for nighttime, the time to sleep, the time to dream, the time to rest your sleepy head.

Nighttime is a good time to feel calm and relaxed.

Nighttime is a good time to enjoy comfort and coziness in the safety of your house.

Sometimes, nighttime feels scary to some, but nighttime is a good time for the beauty of dreams, for the quiet moments when the animals of the night do their work, for the hooting, wise, old owl to bring you messages of peace and quiet.

As you get comfortable under your covers and turn your lights down low, listen to this story of an owl that came to an open window to help a little boy and girl feel safe and secure in the nighttime.

You can take a deep breath in and think about what an owl looks like to start the story tonight.

An owl is a bird of prey that has keen eyesight, especially in the dark.

An owl sees all with its all-knowing eyes and hoots a quiet and soothing call into the stars, under the moon.

Breathe in again and, this time, imagine a cozy, little country cottage on the edge of a wood.

Two little children are lying in bed, a brother and a sister.

They have just been tucked in for the night by their parents.

The candles have been blown out, and the children nuzzle under the covers, feeling the pale coldness of moonlight coming through their windowpane.

"I am frightened, Johnnie," the little girl whispered to her brother, who was only slightly older than she.

"I don't like the cold darkness of the night."

She curled up closer to him for comfort, and her brother put his arm around her.

"I know what you mean, Amy," the brother told the sister.

"I am not good at pretending like I am not afraid of this dark at night."

The two children huddled close together.

Every creak of the trees in the wind, every little noise that came up from the settling world around them, gave them a startle.

"I cannot fall asleep, Johnnie.

I am so tired, and every time I am almost asleep, something wakes me from my rest.

What if the sun never comes up again?

What if we have to always live in the dark?"

The little girl felt worried about how it would feel to stay in this cold darkness.

Her brother understood her fears.

"There, there, Amy. Do not worry. I will hold you close, and as we both fall asleep, it will be like no time has passed, and you will wake up with the sun in the morning."

The two of them were still afraid to shut their eyes, listening to all the night noises around them.

Just as Johnnie was about to shut his eyes, he saw something flash in front of the window, like a streak of white.

"What was that?!" He called out, fearful that he had seen something out of the ordinary.

His sister sat up in bed, tugging the covers up to her chin.

"What happened?" she asked.

"I saw something in the window. There it is again."

This time the window blew open, and the flying object that had scared Johnnie was perched on the windowsill.

A large, beautiful owl was sitting still and staring right at them.

It gave out a calming, “Hoo, hoo, hoo.”

The children, who were initially quite frightened by this sudden appearance, were immediately soothed and calmed by the hoot of the owl friend perched in their window.

They were unsure about what to do now that the window was wide open and that there was an unusual and unlikely nocturnal friend visiting them.

“Hello,” Johnnie whispered cautiously.

“Are you an owl?”

The children stared at the owl, who let another calming and direct, ‘Hoo, hoo.’

The children took a deep breath and suddenly felt calmer, hearing the obvious reply from the owl who was answering Johnnie’s question.

“Should we go get mother and father?” Amy inquired.

She had never been so close to an owl before and felt overwhelmed by its beauty and majesty.

"No need to call your parents, children," the owl commented.

"You can talk!"

Johnnie was astonished, and Amy's mouth hung open in surprise.

"But of course I can talk, children. I am the watcher of the night, and I have come to help you feel at ease."

The children looked at the owl perched in the open window and felt peaceful now that they had a friend to talk to who came from the outer world of darkness.

"Light your candle, Johnnie. Go ahead and bring the warm glow back into your room.

It's alright to have a little light at night, especially if you are feeling unsure of the dark."

Johnnie pulled a match out of the matchbox and lit the candle on the nightstand.

The single flame of the candle was a warm and lovely glow that helped the children feel more relaxed and at peace.

The owl hopped into the room and perched on

the end of the bed frame.

“Now, children, I heard that you cannot fall asleep and that you are afraid of the dark hours of the day.”

The children nodded at his comment.

In the calm glow of the candle burning and with this new companion sitting close and offering comfort, the children felt relaxed again, as they had when their parents read them a story just an hour before.

“Yes, I feel so afraid to close my eyes. The dark feels heavy all around me.

I can’t see everything clearly, and it makes me feel scared or sad when the sun is gone.”

Amy explained.

“I feel that way, too,” Johnnie joined in, “like I can’t let go of today to get to tomorrow. Sometimes, I feel afraid I will miss something, even when it’s dark, and the whole world is taking a nap.”

The owl hooted and nodded.

“These feelings are normal, children, and you are allowed to have them.

But do not fear the dark and the night.

There is a whole world of life continuing while you sleep.

I, for instance, am always awake at night.

It is when I am the most productive and effective in my work."

The children listened eagerly to the owl explain.

They both took a deep breath in and felt relief as they let their breath out and sunk deeper into their pillows, watching the owl speak at their feet.

"The night is a wonderful time, and many wonderful things happen when the sun goes down.

And you can always rest assured that the sun will come up again, little Amy.

You will never have to fear an endless night.

And Johnnie, you will only miss out on something if you are too tired to see it and enjoy it.

If you don't allow your body to rest, you will fall asleep in the day instead of the night and miss out on all of the fun adventures you could have with your family and friends."

The owl hooted again, and the children felt a new sense of comfort.

The owl was a friend from the nighttime who was there to help them feel calm and at peace.

You can learn a lot from an owl, they discovered.

It must be why they are always called 'wise' whenever you hear about them.

"I would like you to know, Johnnie and Amy, that even when you are asleep, I will be here to watch over you and help you feel safe and secure in the night hours.

My nest is in the tree that overlooks your cottage, and while I am at rest in the day, you are at play, and when the night comes and you must sleep,

I will care for your cottage and protect your home.

You can always feel safe, even when the dark is here."

"Thank you, owl," Johnnie was grateful for this comforting friend.

He snuggled into his pillows and blankets.

“Yes, thank you,” responded Amy, who also snuggled into bed.

The owl hopped across the covers and blew out the candle.

“Rest well, children. I will be just outside your window, should you feel afraid of the dark again.”

And with that, the owl hopped on the windowsill and pulled the window close with his beak.

They heard his ‘hoo hoo’ as he flew delicately up into the night.

“Goodnight, Amy. Sleep tight.”

Johnnie told his sister as he fell asleep right away.

“Goodnight, Johnnie. Sweet dreams,” she yawned as she passed into sleep.

That night the two children dreamed of an owl at the foot of their bed, and when they woke up the next day, they felt a new sense of peace and security, knowing that the night owl was going to watch over them and help them to feel safe.

May the owl of your night protect you as you sleep and teach you that there is nothing to fear.

Now you can rest, now you can dream.

Snuggle in tight and sweet dreams!

GRANDPA HEINZ AND THE MERMAID

Tamara sits at the dining table with her grandparents - it's supper time. Grandpa Heinz once again tells the best stories. He used to be a sailor and experienced a lot. Granny Helene tells him over and over again he should not forget the food. But Grandpa Heinz is so busy that he does not come to dinner.

He talks of sea monsters, mermaids and waves as tall as houses. "You're going to spin your sailor's yarn again!" Granny Helene says. "This is not a sailor's yarn, Leni!" Opa Heinz says. "Listen to me for once." "Oh," Grandma Helene grins. "You only give the little boy a fuss."

After dinner, Grandpa Heinz proposes a walk on the beach. "Oh Heinz," says Granny Helene. "It's raining." But Grandpa Heinz is not deterred. "It almost stopped already. Plus, there's clothing for every weather," he says, holding out the rain jacket to Tamara. "We'll be back in half an hour. Will you make us some hot tea? "He asks before Tamara and he walks out the door. And Granny Helene shakes her head and says what she always says: "You stubborn goat. Of course, I'll make tea for you. You should not get any snuff. "

It is uncomfortable weather. The sea is rough. But the rain has almost stopped. The rough sea reminds Grandpa Heinz of stormy seafaring and he starts to talk. The beginning of the story leaves Tamara quiet.

"I remember a seafaring trip that your

grandfather would hardly have survived. It was a long time ago. I was still a young lad myself and did not go to sea much. The sea was even rougher than today and it stormed out of all the heavenly gates. The waves hit the cutter and the whole ship rocked back and forth. Some of the mariners were already afraid that the cutter would be full of water. The waves hit so high.

It was already dark and the rain whipped us in the face. In the dark, we had lost sight and feared walking on a sandbar keel. The best Kieker did not help you in the storm, you know? "Tamara looks questioningly at Opa Heinz: "Kieker?" "Yes," says Opa Heinz. "This is a pair of binoculars. And before you ask, running a keel means the ship is stalling. "Tamara nods wide-eyed and with her mouth open.

Then Opa Heinz continues: "Eventually I did not even believe that we would arrive home safely. We did not even know which direction we needed to go. The storm continued to grow and I no longer saw the hand in my eyes.

Something suddenly shone in the water. At the light, I saw a little girl. Potz Blitz, I thought a stowaway had gone overboard and wanted to make my way to the bell. Then I saw the girl jump out of the water.

I could not believe my eyes. She jumped out of

the water and into it again. Like a dolphin. But I tell you, that was not a dolphin. And it was not a little girl either. When I jumped out of the water, I recognized a huge fin. I'm sure that was a mermaid.

Again and again, she jumped in the air and turned, until I understood that we should follow her. She swam ahead and shone the safe way into the harbor. This little mermaid has saved our lives! But then I never saw her again. Grandma Helene never believed me. But it is the truth."

Tamara looks at Opa Heinz with an open mouth: "I believe you, Grandpa. How did she look?" "Like a little girl. You could not see too much in the dark. I mean she had blond hair and a huge caudal fin. It was really fast - faster than any boat I knew by then."

The rain has stopped and the sea has calmed down. A gentle breeze blows from the water and Tamara eagerly listens to every word that comes out of Grandpa Heinz's mouth.

What they do not know is that the little mermaid from Grandpa Heinz needs his help this time. And right now. Her name is Amelie. At that time, she told Grandpa Heinz the safe way to the harbor. Now she needs help.

Only a few hours ago she had been playing

with the fish at the bottom of the lake. Then the sea freshened up and Amelie realized that she had swum farther out than she wanted.

For such a brave little mermaid that's not a problem, you might think. But even for mermaids, the rough seas can be dangerous. Amelie swam toward the local cave vault, so she was not watching properly and a current seized her. She lost her footing and poked her head against a rock. Unconsciously, she was flushed to the beach and the tide set in.

It is the same beach where Grandpa Heinz and Tamara go for a walk. But the two are still too far away to help Amelie. However, a mermaid on land will not last long.

Amelie wakes up and realizes that she is ashore. The ebb has pushed the sea far back. She wriggles like a fish on dry land, but she does not get on well. She was able to go a short distance. But the sea is much too far away due to the ebb.

Discouraged, she gives up and bursts into tears. "Why is this happening to me? I've never done any harm. "She cries."Oh darling, that has nothing to do with it." A voice suddenly says. Amelie swallows and wipes away her tears. But she sees nothing. "I'm up here," says the voice.

Now Amelie sees a little fairy with beautiful wings flapping around her. “What are you?” Amelie asks. “Well, what does it look like? I am a fairy godmother. To be more specific - your fairy godmother. But you do not have much to do as a fairy of a mermaid, “she smiles.

“Fairies do not exist!” Amelie says. “They are only in fairy tales.” The fairy looks at Amelie confused: “Oh dear. And that comes from a mermaid? Do you know that mermaids are just as mythical as fairies? “

Amelie shakes her head: “No, there are many of us in the sea. We’re not mythical creatures. “The fairy touches her head: “Oh honey, what are they teaching you down there?” Then she makes two fists and holds them against her hips: “No matter, what’s important now is that we get you back into the water. And fast!”

“But how are you going to help me? You are far too small to take me back to the sea.” Amelie says disappointed and close to tears again. “Sweetheart,” says the fairy. “That has nothing to do with size. Even little ones can help! “

Then the fairy thinks: “Hmm, what was the spell for a stranded mermaid? You’ll have to forgive me. I’m out of practice. Most of the time you’re in the water and I’m ashore. What was that again?”

Then she waves her wand and murmurs a few words. The next moment the ground under Amelie begins to fill with water. The water becomes deeper and deeper, until Amelie is completely submerged. The only problem is that the water is only around Amelie. She is swimming in a soap bubble now.

The fairy exhales sadly, “That’s not it,” she says. Then she raises an eyebrow and says, “But we have gained time. Technically speaking, you are back in the water. “Amelie nods, happy to feel water again.

But as much as the little fairy thinks, she does not come up with the spell. “It’s getting pretty dark,” she says. “I’ll light up first.” She waves her wand again and a small light floats next to her. “At least we can see now.”

A few meters further down the beach are Grandpa Heinz and Tamara. When Tamara discovers the light, she excitedly points to it: “Look, grandpa. The light you have been talking about. “Opa Heinz scratches his head: “No, that’s just a lantern. That’s just someone walking.” “But they aren’t moving at all,” Tamara exclaims excitedly. She pulls Grandpa Heinz’s hand. “Come on Grandpa. This is your mermaid!”

Grandpa Heinz wonders if Granny Helene was right after all. Maybe he should not have told the story. Maybe he just filled Tamara’s head with nonsense?

Suddenly, he sees his mermaid floating on the beach in a bubble of water. He stands stiff as a stick: “What, but what?” He says, staring at Amelie. Tamara is quite outraged: “Yes grandpa, you see? I told you. Is that the mermaid who saved you? “Amelie recognizes Grandpa Heinz again.”You’ve gotten older,” she says. “But I recognize you!”

Before the fairy could hear that, she’s already flapping her wings at Grandpa Heinz and punching his nose with her little fists: “Stop!” she exclaims. “You will not touch Amelie, otherwise you will have to deal with me!” Grandpa Heinz carefully reaches for the fairy: “It’s all right. I will do nothing to her. We know each other.” The fairy looks over at Amelie surprised: “Is that true?” Amelie nods.

Grandpa Heinz comes closer to Amelie: “So your name is Amelie?” he asks. Then he points to Tamara. “This is my granddaughter Tamara.” Amelie greets Tamara, who has now stopped babbling and stands with her mouth open. “You are beautiful!” Tamara says and Amelie thanks her.

Grandpa Heinz extends his hand to the water and says: “I could never thank you enough. You saved my life! “At that moment, the fairy hits his hand: “Stay away from my water.” Then she waves her forefinger: “Touching the shape with your paws is forbidden. Now you go. We have work to do!"

The fairy flutters to Amelie and tries hard to push the bubble of water. But it does not move. Amelie is too heavy. "I'll help you," says Opa Heinz and just wants to push, as the fairy cries out: "NO! I said do not touch! "Grandpa Heinz stops.

"If you touch the bubble of water, it will burst, or worse!" The little fairy is just catching her breath as she sees little Tamara push the bubble of water out of the corner of her eye. "But how is that possible?" the fairy asks.

Amelie nods to the fairy, "It's alright. Tamara is my soulmate. As I had felt with Heinz at that time, I now feel with her. And I will eventually feel it with their children." Tamara pushes the little mermaid back into the sea.

As Amelie is back in the sea, she jumps around happily in the waves. Then she comes up and waves to Tamara: "Thank you, dear Tamara. We will definitely meet again! But now I have to go back," she says, turning around and disappearing in the waves.

When Tamara turns around, the fairy is gone as well. Grandpa Heinz stands further back on the beach and beckons Tamara. "Come on, little one, we have to go back too. Granny Helene is already waiting for us with the tea."

When they arrive home Tamara tells them about the water bubble. The story gushes out of her: "And then I pushed the mermaid back into the sea. She waved at me once more and then disappeared. Even the fairy was gone then." Granny Helene strokes her cheek: "Well, you have experienced a real adventure. But now the tea is ready. Don't let it go cold."

After Tamara has gone to bed, Grandma Helene looks at Grandpa Heinz and smiles: "What did you do with her? She talked until she fell asleep. The sailor's yarn that she spins does not fit anymore." Grandpa Heinz only smiles back and nods: "There's so much out there. And stories want to be told. Let her dream!"

Then Grandma Helene and Grandpa Heinz go to bed. And Grandpa Heinz is happy that he now has someone who believes in him and shares his stories with him. Even if it will remain a secret between the two. Tamara and he know there's a little mermaid out there called Amelie, who will always watch over them at sea.

THE DEEP BLUE SEA

Here is a story of the blue ocean. Join me as we explore all that it has to offer. Together, we will sail the seven seas and find the treasure that is hidden under the waves. Remember to follow along to the best of your ability and to let your imagination run wild. Whatever world you imagine is yours to explore. So long as you swim behind me, I will show you the way.

Imagine now the vastness of the ocean. Do you even know how much water there is in the sea? It's impossible to tell how much there really is. Have you ever been to the beach? Do you remember how the waves went in and out and how the water came crashing down at your feet?

Even if you have never gone to the beach, you can still imagine it: the sand, the waves and the sun. All these things are just a very tiny, tiny part of the bigger picture that is the ocean. Each beach has its own story, and all of these stories combine to form what we know as the ocean.

Now, the next time you go to the beach, I hope you remember to clean up after yourself. The beach isn't a garbage can. There are thousands of different animals that live in the water and call the ocean home. They do not like having to swim through trash. How would you feel if somebody dumped a bunch of smelly socks on your bed? You probably wouldn't like it very much!

The surface of the ocean is like a great big bowl

of water. Only it's a bowl that goes on for miles and miles, and is deeper than anything else on earth. Imagine swimming in a pool that could hold the biggest skyscraper under the water. That is the ocean, and it's where our next story takes place.

Imagine now a beautiful blue ocean. Waves come crashing down at the shore and it goes on as far as the eye can see. Imagine that you can hear the crashing of the waves and the calling of the sea birds as they fly overhead. Maybe there are boats on the docks, getting ready for a day at sea. Or maybe there is nothing out there. And it's just one big, calm blue ocean.

Imagine that you have a bird's eye view of the water from above. From up here, you can see just how big the ocean is. Imagine that all you can see is an endless blue of water and waves. It's very peaceful, isn't it? There are no people here, no roads, and no houses. It's just a big shade of watery blue. Right now, you are just floating above the water. You look down, and you see your shoelaces hanging in the air.

The water looks perfectly peaceful. There are small waves, tiny waves, and great, big waves that come crashing down. Then, from the corner of your eye, you see something strange. It looks like a wave, but it's different from before. Water shoots out high and almost splashes you. What is it?

This is no wave. As you look closely, you can see that there is a shadow there, moving along with the water—a shadow that gets bigger and bigger. And then you realize that it is no shadow either. There is something large right below your feet. You gasp. It's a whale! And it's not just any whale, but a huge humpback whale. She is very happy to see you and leaps through the water with all her might, sending a huge splash of water in your direction. How such a large animal can leap in the air is a mystery.

Our whale friend is happy because she has just given birth to a baby whale. That's right; she's a mama. And what's more, she wants you to see her baby. But we can't see the baby whale from up here. We have to go down and submerge ourselves into the water. We are going to get a little wet, but in the end, it will be worth it.

Don't be afraid of the water. It's just water. Sometimes, humans get scared of the water because they don't know how to swim, and they think they might drown. But here in the realm of our imagination, we don't have to worry about that. Let yourself go and follow me into the water.

Slowly, lower your body into the water. First, your shoes touch the surface and are slowly taken by the sea. You feel the water filling up your shoes and socks, but that is okay. Next, your legs and pants go down. They start to feel heavy. But that is also okay because underwater, you don't weigh a thing.

The water is up to your waist now. See? It wasn't so bad. But we still can't see the baby whale from here. So, we continue to go down. Next, the water starts to go up to your chest. You are completely soaked now. You might as well go all the way, right? Your arms go down, and you can feel your hand pushing away at the heavy water. It's almost like being stuck in a really big bubble.

Now, we are up to our neck in water. We need our eyes to see, so our heads must also go down. Slowly, you feel the water rise again, rising over your neck and up to your chin. It goes further up, touching your lips and then your nose. You are underwater, but you can still breathe. It's easy. Just for today, you are a fish.

The water goes up to your eyes and ears, and you can no longer see the blue sky. Instead, you see the darkness. But don't be afraid. It takes a while for your eyes to get used to it.

Soon, you find that you can see just fine. Above, you can see how the sun reflects on top of the waves. You see the light up there, where the sun should be, but we aren't interested in it. We want to see the baby whale, so we must go deeper still. Remember not to be scared of the darkness.

As you continue to go deeper into the ocean, all you can see is blue. You hear a scary sound that sounds like a monster howling. It is a dark and mysterious sound, like the ocean is whispering its secrets to you. You have never heard anything like it. Your ears need to get used to the pressure under the sea. All around you, you hear a strange bubbling sound, like if the water is boiling. But don't worry; that's just the sound of the water around your ears.

The same scary sounds continue. You feel motionless and completely alone. But you aren't alone down here. Those scary noises that you hear are the whales. They talk to each other through song. It is the song of the ocean. The mama whale must be nearby because you can hear her song getting louder and louder.

She is, in fact, right below you. And to the side of her, you can see a smaller whale who refuses to leave her side. This is Amy, the baby humpback whale. Like you, this is her first time entering the ocean. She is a little scared. But just like you, she is eager to see what more the ocean can offer.

Amy pokes her head under her mama's fins, and she waves hello. She is a very curious whale, despite just being born a few moments ago.

As your eyes get accustomed to the darkness underwater, you notice that you are not alone. All around, you can see other whale families nursing their young. The whales all sing their song like a chorus. If you haven't guessed, the whales all meet here to have their babies.

Soon, they will have to travel south where the water is warmer. This will be Amy's first big migration, and she is very excited about it. At the same time, Amy must say goodbye to all the friends that she made at the whale colony.

"Why must we leave?" Amy asked her mama.

"It's because we are whales, and that's what we do," she said. "Don't you worry. Migration is fun, and I promise that you will meet lots of new friends."

"But I want to stay here!" said Amy. One day when she is older, she will understand. And she, too, will make the journey to the south. But now, it is time to return home with her mama. One by one, you watch as the other whales disappear deeper into the ocean as they go on their own journey. The song of the whales gets harder and harder to hear.

The mama whale beckons to you with her enormous fin and asks you to follow them on their journey. That way, Amy will not feel so lonely. The ocean can be a big, scary place for a baby whale. And though her mama is the size of a city bus, Amy is much smaller. Being small can be scary sometimes, especially when the ocean is so vast.

The journey will be long, and it will be difficult. Mama whale and her calf start to move away with the others. They are headed south, where the water is warmer. On the way there, they must stay close together because it is safer that way. A little whale, like Amy, could easily get lost. A few of the other whales sing their song to signal that they are all together. This way, the whales can travel in numbers so that they are safer.

And though the big ocean is scary, traveling in numbers makes it seem less scary. You are doing your part by following the whales. Amy feels safer already and is eager to see what else she might see in the ocean.

"Be careful not to swim too far," said Mama whale. "Stay close to me and the other whales. And be nice to everyone you meet."

"Yes, mama," said Amy as she clings tightly to her mother's side.

On such a long journey like this, it is only natural to see other fish in the water. Amy will meet many different species of fish, all in different shapes and sizes. Some are friends and others are less than friendly.

Because of her size, many other types of fish are scared of her. But that is silly because Amy would never hurt a fly. She is big because she has a big heart. And she is glad that somebody like you is there with her on this journey.

Oops. I made a mistake. I just referred to Amy as a fish! But Amy is no fish. It's true, she lives in the ocean just like fish, but she's a whale. She swims as any fish might do, but she is also very different from them. Whales belong to the mammal family of the animal kingdom. This means that they are warm-blooded and use lungs to breathe.

You may have heard about dolphins. They are also mammals. Every other type of whale is a mammal, as well. Aren't they wonderful creatures? In fact, you and I are both mammals! Just like whales, we need air to survive. And when we were babies, we all drank mamas' milk. It's a mammal thing.

But where do whales get their air? Under the ocean, they are surrounded by water, are they not? The answer is quite obvious once you think about it. Just like you and me, whales have noses or nostrils that they use to inhale air. But their noses are on the top of the heads, and they are called blowholes.

Amy and her mama are about to go up for some much-needed air. They have to do this every once in a while. Like you and me, they have to hold their breath underwater. But unlike you and me, a whale can hold their breath for a very long time.

Our whale friends go up toward the surface and make a big splash as they breach for a nice long breath. When you think about it, whales are very similar to us. We live in a house, and they live in the ocean. And since the ocean is their home, we must be careful not to pollute it; we need to keep it clean.

Whales swim for their entire lives. To us it sounds strange, but to them it is natural. Swimming is the way to be. They just have to keep swimming until they reach the south. They sing their songs as they go and talk to each other through signals.

It is Amy's first migration, and she is feeling a little bored. It's such a big ocean with so much to see, but all that she can see is the deep blue of the water. And swimming gets tiresome. Before long, Amy is crying and complaining, just like any other baby might. When you were a little smaller, you also probably cried and complained a lot.

"Mama, I'm bored!" pouted Amy. She wanted to make friends and swim on her own, but her mama wouldn't let her.

"Not now, Amy," said her mama. "Wait until

we get to the coast, then you will have some fun, I promise."

But Amy didn't know what her mama was talking about. She wanted to have fun now and not later. But her mama promised that things would change for the better.

"I'm hungry!" groaned Amy again. This time, her mama had no choice but to listen to her. When a baby whale is hungry, and there is no food around, her mama has to squirt some of her milk into the water so that the baby can drink.

And that is exactly what her mama did.

"YUM!" said Amy. And soon, she fell asleep at her mama's side. When a baby whale decides to sleep, they get really close to their mama, and they swim as one. Whales can sleep when they swim, surprisingly!

When the ocean is deep, there is not much to see. But when the ocean floor is clearly visible, there is so much to see. At lunchtime, a whale might decide to swim toward the coast, where the majority of fish like to hang out.

When Amy woke up from her nap, she was pleasantly surprised. The ocean suddenly changed colors from a deep, dark blue to a see-through baby-blue color. There was more light now because the sun was closer to the floor of the ocean. They had made it to the coast, and Amy couldn't be more excited.

In the distance, you could already see trees growing underwater. But these aren't ordinary trees. There are ocean plants. Some of them are green; others are yellow and look like long chains that reach the water's surface. Still, others are colorful, like the rainbow.

"Be careful, Amy. Things aren't always what they seem," said mama whale.

"Okay, I promise I'll be careful!" said Amy.

Now that they were closer to the coast, her mamma was more comfortable with letting her swim by herself. You decided to follow the excited baby whale and see where she would take you. Amy headed straight for a vast coral reef formation.

Coral reefs are among the most beautiful things you can see in the ocean. The one that Amy has spotted is the most colorful thing you have ever seen. There are several different colors of white, blue, yellow, green and bright red corals.

These corals are, in fact, living organisms. They are not quite plants, but they are not quite animals either. To you and me, they look like colorful rocks with different tentacles and hairy arms. Coral reefs are home to many different species of fish. Amy is sure to make friends if she looks for them here.

Amy sees the beautiful patterns on the coral and heads straight for them. You follow close behind her, taking in all the different colors and the fish that swim by. Coral reefs are tiny little communities where all sorts of fish, crabs, and other sea critters come together.

You see striped fish, fish with polka dots, and fish with bright colors. There are so many of them, and they keep coming from different directions. You can also see a seahorse and its family floating by. Above you, Amy, the curious whale, goes for a breath of fresh air and then comes down in a dive.

As she dives down, she scares almost all the fish away. But this is just her way of saying hello. Amy doesn't yet understand that her size is scary to others. It's not her fault that she was born a whale. But sometimes, it is easy to judge based on appearances. It isn't right, but it happens very often.

"Where have all the fish gone?" asked Amy as she dipped her nose next to the closest coral.

"Wow! These are so pretty."

She had completely forgotten her mama's advice about being careful and that things are not always what they appear. Instead, she went around, sticking her nose into the coral reefs, trying to see if she could meet a new friend.

"Ouch! That hurt!" She said out loud, rubbing her face. You turn in time to see what happened, but all you see is a strange plant with many dancing tentacles. Just a second ago, Amy was sticking her nose inside it.

"That happens," said a voice coming behind the coral. "You need to be careful around these animals. They are called anemones, and they are my home."

"Huh? Who said that?" asked Amy.

"Down here!" said the voice from before.

Amy looked down, and there was a small orange fish looking back at her. The fish had white shiny stripes, and it looked very friendly.

"I'm a clownfish, and my name is Marlo," said the orange fish. "Nice to meet ya!"

Amy quickly forgot all about the sting. Finally, she found a new friend.

"Hi! I'm Amy," she said. "I'm looking for an

adventure!"

"Hi, Amy!" said Marlo. "Boy, you sure are big!"

"I'm not that big. You should see my mama!"

"If you came here looking for adventure, you found the right place," said Marlo, gesturing with his fins at the reef.

And he was right. The coral reef was full of little fish swimming around like a big aquarium. There was so much to see that Amy didn't know where to start.

"This is my home," said Marlo, pointing at the yellowish tentacles that gave Amy a nasty sting. "It only stung you because it thought you were trying to hurt me."

"That thing is alive?" asked Amy with a curious look on her face.

"Sure is!" said Marlo. "In fact, the entire coral reef is alive and well."

You see, Marlo's home is part of a larger habitat called an ecosystem. The ocean is full of them, and everything works together in a delicate balance. When somebody throws trash in the ocean, the ecosystem is disrupted, and things don't work very well. The ocean gets dirty, and some of the fish die.

"Would you like to meet my friends?" Marlo asked.

Amy was super excited, and she couldn't help it.

"Yes! Please, please, please introduce me to your friends!"

Marlo swam off to a different part of the reef, where it was quieter.

"My friends might be a little scared when they see you, but don't worry. I'll tell them you are friendly!"

Amy tried to follow Marlo, but she was too big. She accidentally bumped into the coral reef and made a big commotion.

"Oops, sorry!" said Amy.

"OUCH!"

The coral reef started to talk. And then it started to move. But it was no coral reef. Amy didn't know what it was. It changed colors and started moving around. At first, it looked like a plastic bag, but Amy saw that it was moving around with tentacles.

"Oh, hi, Ronnie," said Marlo. "Amy, this is Ronnie, the octopus. Ronnie, this is Amy, the whale."

The octopus changed colors from purple to tan, to blue, and then to green. Amy had never seen such a creature before in her life. She thought the octopus was the prettiest thing she'd seen in the water.

But Ronnie wasn't so sure about her size. Amy was really big, and she was a little scary too. After she bumped into him, Ronnie didn't know if it was safe to come out. Instead, he swam inside a little hole on the side of the coral reef.

"Is it safe to come out yet?" he asked Marlo. "I don't want to be bumped again!"

Amy knew the octopus didn't mean it, but he still hurt her feelings. She wanted to be their friend, but instead, she messed everything up.

Marlo tried to explain that Amy was friendly, but the poor little scared octopus wouldn't come out of his hole.

"She gave me a real fright!" said Ronnie, the octopus. "I thought a shark was going to eat me!"

But then Marlo corrected him.

“Ronnie, this is Amy; she’s a whale. She doesn’t eat octopus!”

Despite their differences, Amy and Ronnie the octopus were able to get along. Things were a little confusing at first, but they quickly got sorted out. Before long, Ronnie, Marlo and Amy were all swimming together and having a good time.

Amy was big, but she was careful not to be rough with her new friends. And her new friends took her to wide-open spaces so that she wouldn’t bump into things by accident. For Amy, it was the first time that anyone helped her play because of her size, and she was grateful for it.

The other fish who lived on the reef took notice of the baby whale playing with some of the residents. Some of them were scared at first, like Ronnie. But they were having so much fun, playing tag and hide and seek that soon they forgot about her size and were no longer scared of Amy.

Every time she had to go up to get air, the other fish would follow and see who could make it the farthest up before she dived underwater again. They made a game out of it, and fun was had by all.

Amy felt what friendship was for the first time in her life. She adored her new friends, and they adored her. Everyone wanted to meet her, talk to her and be around her. She was quite popular because the other fish had never even talked to a whale before.

There was Ronnie the octopus, Marlo the clownfish, Henry the seahorse, Arthur the crab and Selena the pufferfish. Each of her new friends was unique in their own way. And just like Amy was large, some of the other fish were strange.

Selena the pufferfish looked funny and would occasionally blow up like a balloon. Ronnie the octopus had a thing for spitting black ink everywhere, and Henry the seahorse had a bad case of the burps.

Even so, Amy was able to look past these small things. If they could accept her for being a whale, then she could accept them for being the way they were.

After what seemed like forever, you heard the same whale songs from before. Amy looked in the distance and saw that her mama was waiting for her near the surface of the water. Uh, oh. It was time to say goodbye to her friends.

Amy was sad, but at the same time, she was excited to continue with the journey south. She knew that she would return to see her friends at the coral reef. She said goodbye to each and every one of them. They all said their goodbyes and told her that they couldn't wait until the next time she came to visit.

And with that, Amy swam back to her mama and the rest of the pack. Even though she had plenty of fun with her new friends, it felt good to be back with the other whales. Her mama waited for her and gave her a big hug when she returned.

"Did you have fun, Amy?"

"I sure did!"

"I know you like making friends, Amy. But remember that the ocean is big and sometimes scary. Remember to be careful every time."

Amy wasn't sure what her mom meant. So far, all the fish she met were very friendly. She was the one who scared all the little fish away. But Amy knew that her mama was wise and that it was better to listen.

"Amy, not every fish you meet will be your friend. In the coastal waters, we need to watch out for sharks."

"What are sharks, mama?" asked Amy.

"They are big, scary fish with big teeth. If you get

too close, they will try to eat you."

Amy gulped. She didn't like the idea of being eaten.

The coast was beautiful. Amy took large, big breaths of air every chance she could get. The air was fresh, and the sun felt warm against her skin. Below her, she could see tiny critters walking along the ocean floor. Every once in a while, a tiny fish zoomed by.

Every time Amy saw a new fish, she asked her mama what it was. Being a baby whale was often confusing. Amy didn't know which fish were friends and which ones were bad.

A school of fish swam by, and Amy tried to say hi. But the fish were moving too fast, and they didn't look like they wanted to talk. She was a little sad about it, but she remembered her mama's words. Not every fish she would meet would be her friend.

From then on, Amy was only interested in the fish that looked friendly. If they didn't look nice, she wouldn't talk to them. And boy, are there lots of angry fish in the ocean. They don't say hi; they don't stop to enjoy the water. They just zoom by like it's none of their business.

Amy saw many kinds of fish that were like that.

Some of them swam so fast that she couldn't even see them.

"What was that?" She asked when a jet of bubbles flew past her.

"That's a swordfish," said her mama. "It's one of the fastest fish in the world."

And boy, was her mama right. The swordfish swam through the water like a bullet. Amy wished she could be that fast. Then she could win against everyone at racing. She always came in last because of how big and slow she was.

"Mama, I hear something," said Amy. "What is it?"

What Amy was hearing seemed to come from above the water. It didn't sound at all like whale-speak. The sound was higher, and she could barely hear it. But there it was.

"Why don't you go up and see for yourself?" asked her mama.

Her mama went up for air, and Amy followed her closely behind. This time, her mama got some speed, and when it was time to get air, she flopped her tail in the air and made a big splash. It all happened so fast that Amy didn't notice it, but her mama went up in the air!

"Wow!" She said. "How did you do that?"

"It's easy," said her mom. "All you have to do is lift your fins like this, and then throw your body in the air!"

Amy tried her best to jump like her mama, but she couldn't go as high. The world above the water was so different from the ocean. And in the few seconds that Amy saw above water, all she could see was blue from the sky.

"Did you see them?" asked her mama.

"I didn't see anything!"

Her mama carefully nudged Amy in the right direction. She could still hear the sound from before, and it was getting louder.

"Go on, take a look," said her mama.

Amy went up to the surface to get air and poke her head out just a little bit from the water. What she saw completely astonished her. There, on a group of rocks, she could see hundreds of sea lions.

"Mama, what are they?" said Amy after she went back in the water. "They are so strange!"

“They are called sea lions. They live both in the water and on land.”

Wow! thought Amy. How nice it must be to live on land and in the water. It was like having the best of both worlds. She wanted to get closer, but she didn’t know if it was okay.

Then without warning, she could see a whole bunch of the sea lions jumping from the rocks and entering the water. There was a small splash, and then three of them jumped, then six, and then nine.

“It must be feeding time for them,” said her mama. “But don’t worry. They only eat small fish.”

Amy was intrigued. And after asking her mama, she went to go get a closer look. What strange creatures! A minute ago, they were lying on the rocks, and then the next, they were diving like excellent swimmers.

“Hi!” said Amy to the sea lion closest to her. The startled creature turned around fast to see her and shook its whiskers at her. Was Amy talking to her?

“Hello,” he said. “Can I help you?”

“My name is Amy, and I want to be friends with you!” she said.

The sea lion seemed to think about it for a while. It wasn't every day that a baby whale asked you to be her friend. But after a while, the sea lion thought it was a super idea.

"Okay!" he said. "My name is Austin!"

Amy and Austin played tag underwater. And when Austin needed to get some air, she would jump in the air with him. They took turns jumping in and out of the water. Her mama was watching them closely the entire time just in case something went wrong.

To her surprise, Austin was very friendly. Once he got comfortable around her, it was all fun and games. They swam around the rocks, but Amy had to be careful not to get stuck. Austin even invited some of his sea lion friends, and they all played a game of hide-and-seek in between the rocks. Amy was always the first one out, but she didn't seem to mind.

She was having such a good time, but then she heard the familiar song of the other whales in her pack. It sounded like something was happening. And it must have been true because her mama came rushing to her side.

"I think I have to go now, guys!" Amy said to her sea lion friends. They said their goodbyes, and

Amy promised to return one day.

"Amy, I have bad news," said her mama. "One of the whales has spotted sharks in the area. We have to leave the coast for now."

"Sharks?" said Amy. "Are we in danger?"

"Everything is okay," her mama reassured her. "We just have to continue our journey south now. Okay?"

Amy said that she understood, and before long, they were swimming away from the coast. Slowly, the whales made their way off the coast and into open water. The ocean got darker again, and before long, Amy could no longer see the ocean floor.

She missed her sea lion friends, but she was happy to be with her mama again. Most of all, she was glad to be away from the sharks.

"Mama, what's that?"

Amy had spotted something shiny in the water below them. To her, it looked as if the sun was reflecting on something, but she didn't know what. There are not many things under the ocean that shine like that. What could it be? It wasn't a shark, was it?

Her mama saw it, too, and said that it was probably nothing. But that wasn't enough for Amy. She wanted to know what it was.

"Amy, you get back here this instant!" said her mom.

"I'm just going to have a little peek."

Amy dove deeper into the water and made her way to the shiny object. Below her, the water was a deep dark blue, and she couldn't tell what else was below. It looked scary. She was diving deeper than she had ever gone before. Something told her that she had to go down.

"Amy, come back! It isn't safe!" Her mama raced behind her, and another whale followed.

The shiny thing got bigger and bigger, and Amy could see an even larger shadow around it. The shadow was moving but very slowly. It seemed to be struggling.

"Mama, look!"

"I told you not to go down this far—oh, dear!"

Her mama saw the same thing she did. The shiny thing was a piece of plastic wrapped around its neck. It was a six-pack soda ring, and the turtle couldn't escape.

"We need to get help, mama!" said Amy.

Her mama started signaling to the other whales what had happened. In the meantime, another whale helped push the turtle higher up toward the surface so that it wouldn't sink. Amy didn't know what to do. Her fins were too fat and meaty to help the turtle out. The other whales were all too big.

"It's going to be okay," her mama said to calm her down. "One of the other whales has spotted a swordfish that can help us."

"A swordfish? You mean one of those rude fish that zoomed by her earlier and didn't even say hello?"

"You would be surprised what some fish can do if you ask them nicely."

When the swordfish arrived, Amy felt all her worry go away. It turned into excitement instead. The turtle was going to be rescued after all!

"Marlin's the name," said the swordfish. "I can have this turtle out in no time!"

She watched in amazement as the swordfish used his pointy bill to rip the plastic apart. Marlin shook his entire body side to side to free the poor sea turtle. All the movement kicked up so many bubbles that Amy could no longer see what was happening.

But when everything cleared up, she could see the piece of plastic dangling from the end of Marlin's bill. The sea turtle was freed!

"Don't mention it; don't mention it," said the swordfish to the sea turtle and then disappeared into deeper waters. The turtle was a little shook up but could swim just fine after it was freed from the plastic. It said its thanks and swam off.

Then it was just the whales continuing their journey to the south. Amy was so happy that she spotted the turtle and that they were able to get the help it needed.

What an amazing place the ocean was. In the ocean, Amy learned that nothing is what it seems. Just because she was a big whale, it didn't mean that she wasn't a good friend. And just because a fish looks ugly on the outside, it doesn't mean they are ugly on the inside.

When she first saw the piece of plastic, Amy thought that it was a shiny jewel. But in the end, it was just plastic. But it was a good thing that she saw it. After that day, Amy learned to listen to her mama's advice that not everything is what it seems.

This is the story of a boy named Johnnie who gets to escape from a scary storm with the help of a group of playful dinosaurs and a backpack filled with supplies. This is a great story to read to your child when they are afraid of a storm. It will help them to process their feelings about the weather and their feelings of bravery. The story is imaginative and places imagination as one of the key tools for anyone to use when they are scared.

Once upon a time, there was a boy named Johnnie. Johnnie was in his bed scared, since there was a storm going on outside. He was wondering when the storm was going to end. His mother said that the storm would pass over their town quickly and that he should get some sleep. Unfortunately, he couldn't get any sleep because of the storm.

Johnnie kept listening to the tick-tock-tick-tock of the clock. The night seemed to go on forever. Every minute the storm raged on felt like hours and hours to him. He could hear the crashing sound of the thunder outside and the flash of the lightning made him duck under his covers scared. Sometimes, the thunder was so loud it would make his windows shake.

He wondered if he should go to his parent's room, but he was trying to be a big brave boy. He felt that big brave boys wouldn't crawl into their parents' beds because they were afraid of the stormy weather outside. His dad had even helped him to prepare for the weather in case the storm lasted all night. They had filled a backpack with supplies, games, and toys. He had even snuck some comic books into the bag when his father wasn't looking. The backpack was now hidden under the blankets with him. He clutched tightly onto the Panda bear that he had owned since he was a very young boy.

His mother made sure that Johnnie had some goodies near his bed. He had a bag of popcorn and some chips to eat in case he got hungry and didn't want to wait for the morning. His mother had told him that sometimes a snack makes her less scared.

He remembered the time when his family had gone camping. Even though it was only last weekend, it seemed like it was long ago. He was supposed to be a brave boy with camping experience. He felt like campers shouldn't be scared of a little storm. But the storm raged on outside.

In his bed, he felt something touch his toes. Then he heard a voice. It whispered under the covers, "Ouch, that hurts." But the noise was drowned out by the noises from outside. Johnnie looked out the window, but it was dark and the storm clouds in the sky blocked out the stars from the sky.

The sound of thunder and the flashes of lightning stopped for just long enough for Johnnie to think to himself, "What was that noise from under the covers?"

He rifled through his backpack looking for his flashlight. He couldn't find it. He must have forgotten to pack it when he was trying desperately to hide the comic books. He freaked out for a second and then remembered that he had left it on the dresser. He knew he would be scared to get out of bed during the storm, but the flashlight would help things be less scary.

He ran over to the dresser and grabbed the flashlight. Just then the crash of thunder and a flash of lightning came from outside and, without any haste, Johnnie ran and jumped back into his bed. He stretched his feet down to the bottom of the sheets and there he felt something rough and sharp at his toes. It seemed to be crawling around his ankles.

"What's in my bed," he wondered aloud.

He knew there was something in his bed, so he peeked inside. Without the flashlight he could barely make anything out, it was so black under the covers, almost as black as the sky outside. However, he did see some tiny little spots that looked like eyes.

He heard a roar come from behind one of his legs.

Johnnie was scared and chewed on his thumbnail, but then he had a thought and remembered that he had the flashlight. He looked under the covers for the sound. In his bed were a bunch of little tiny dinosaurs. But dinosaurs were big and extinct, he thought to himself.

He was obviously wrong because there was a tiny little stegosaurus. It was eating one of his ribbed potato chips from one of the bags he had opened hoping that the snack would help him feel less afraid as his mother had suggested.

Johnnie was confused, but then he said, "Get out of here."

The animal began to say something, and then he heard more noises. He used the flashlight to look around underneath his covers. He saw more shadows and looked for them. First, he saw a triceratops, then a pterodactyl, and then a tyrannosaurus rex. Johnnie wondered how many tiny dinosaurs were in this bed with him.

Johnnie wanted to run away; he was scared but also a little curious. He wondered how there were so many dinosaurs in his bed and where they had come from. He looked under his bed with his flashlight and thought he could see for miles. He thought about hiding but then thought that maybe he should explore this grand land under his covers.

It looked like a different world under his covers and he was frozen with amazement. He felt his heart beating over and over again. Then he felt a tingle as if lightning had zapped his blanket. He could see the lightning in the blanket's sky. He saw the animals chasing each other. He saw an apatosaurus chasing a stegosaurus. He wondered what on earth was going on.

The animals were playing with each other, it seemed. At least that's what Johnnie thought, because plant-eaters were chasing meat-eaters. Suddenly a big brachiosaurus began to run towards Johnnie. He was scared for a minute, but then he remembered that long-necked dinosaurs like the brachiosaur were plant eaters, and there was no way he would hurt him. But Johnnie didn't want to take any chances. He pulled a fire truck out of his backpack and it grew to a tremendous size. Johnnie was able to jump into the front seat and turn on the siren. But the sound hurt his ears.

Dinosaurs began to follow him in the truck, first a brontosaurus and a diplodocus in addition to the brachiosaurus that was following him. But they didn't want to hurt him; they were acting like big friendly dogs that want to play. But Johnnie was scared he might be crushed by their big dinosaur feet.

He gave the truck some gas and it sped forward.

He followed a path under the bed and it soon led to a forest. Before he got to the forest, he stepped on the brake and parked. He put on his new sneakers from his backpack and got out of the truck. He began to run away, blowing a whistle that was also in his backpack. He could hear the trampling of dinosaur feet from behind him.

He held on to his panda tightly and ran. As he ran, the wind blew his hat off of his head. He ran through the forest and tried to escape the animals that were chasing him, but he couldn't seem to stay too far in front of them. He was no longer worried about the storm raging outside his bedroom with all this going on deep inside his bed. He wondered how this even happened.

He could hear the growls of the dinosaurs and their speeding thumping feet behind him. He reached into his backpack. Inside his pack was a pair of roller skates. He decided to stop for a second and put the skates on. He'd be able to get away from these dinosaurs if he was skating, he was a fast skater. But he didn't get too far before he hit a tree root and fell headfirst into the mud. He quickly took off the skates and began to climb the tree. He wondered where his mom and dad were.

He scrambled up the tree trunk. He began to jump from branch to branch and as he was about to reach another one, a brontosaurus came from out of nowhere eating a mouthful of leaves. The brontosaurus looked at him.

Suddenly, from out of nowhere, he heard someone calling his name. He couldn't figure out where the sound was coming from. He raced back to the opening of the bed and threw off the blankets. It was his mom and dad. It was morning; the sun was shining out from the window. His panda was still tucked securely underneath his arm.

"I see you found the surprises we left in your bed. We left those toy dinosaurs for you to find in the dark, figuring it would take your mind off the storm," said his father.

"Toys," Johnnie said confused. They had seemed so real in the dark.

"And I'm very proud of you for stacking them neatly on your dresser," said his mother.

Johnnie didn't remember placing any dinosaurs on the dresser. There were all the dinosaurs that he saw in the land underneath his bed covers. Even if those dinosaurs were stuffed toys, they helped him fight his fear, because the most important thing to do to overcome fears is holding on good friends.

THE TICKLY TIGER

Once upon a time, there was a tiger named Tara. Tara was a very ticklish tiger. Every time someone would touch her, she would laugh and laugh. She would laugh so hard that she could not breathe. Everyone liked to tickle Tara. It would make her laugh and roll around, and they thought that it was very funny. But, Tara did not like being tickled. She did not want other people to tickle her because it was not fun.

So, one day, Tara decided that she did not want to be ticklish anymore. "I don't like tickles!" she told herself. "So, I won't laugh at them anymore! I won't be tickly at all!" And off, Tara went on her day. She went to go on her way through the trees and looked around. All around her, other animals were working very hard on their day. They were searching for food. They were building nests for their babies. They were all going about their day, and Tara was glad. No one was bothering her, and that meant that she would not be tickled!

But, just when she thought she was safe, down came a monkey from a tree. He was very quiet, and Tara did not hear him. He reached down and tickled Tara's sides, holding onto a branch with his tail as he did. Tara roared and then started to laugh. She laughed and laughed and rolled around. "Stop, stop!" she said, laughing as she rolled around the ground.

The monkey laughed at her and kept tickling her. So, Tara took a big, deep breath to try to stop laughing, but she only ended up laughing harder! But, she was not having fun. She did not like to be tickled.

So, when the monkey stopped tickling her, Tara looked at him angrily. "I don't like tickles, Monkey," she said. She frowned and sat down. Her tail swung around behind her, and she was very frustrated that she was not being listened to.

"If you don't like tickles, why did you laugh?" asked Monkey.

"I don't know," said Tara, getting even more frustrated. "But please don't tickle me. I don't want you to tickle me anymore." She didn't know why he didn't want to listen.

Monkey nodded his head when he realized she was being honest. "Okay," he said. "I'm sorry I tickled you! I didn't know that you didn't like being tickled. I thought we were playing." He looked embarrassed that he had been bothering her for so long without knowing it!

Tara nodded back. "Thank you!" she said, and then off she went. That worked, thought Tara.

She was very glad that Monkey had listened to her! She had never thought that she should just say no if she did not want to play with people. She always wanted to make other people happy, but sometimes, she needed to say no for herself, too! And today was one of those days. But, how could she make everyone hear her?

Maybe all she had to do was say what she was thinking so the other animals would listen to her! Maybe if she told enough animals that she didn't like being tickled, they wouldn't tickle her anymore! After all, if someone told her that they didn't like what she was doing to them, she would stop too!

So, off Tara went. Every time that she heard an animal coming up behind her, she would stop and look at them. "Excuse me!" she would tell them. "I don't like being tickled. Please leave me alone!"

First, she saw a snake that tried to tickle her. He was very surprised to hear that she did not like being tickled. "Why didn't you say so?" he asked. He felt very bad because he liked to sneak up and tickle her. He thought it was a game too! But, when Tara told him no more, he nodded his head and agreed. If she did not want to be tickled, then he would not tickle her!

Tara kept going and saw her best friend, Trina Tiger. Trina also tried to tickle Tara, but Tara said,

"No! Please leave me alone!" She looked at Trina angrily.

Trina seemed surprised. "Don't you like being tickled?" she asked. "I thought everyone liked to be tickled, and I thought that you liked being tickled more than anyone else! After all, you always sit there and laugh when you are tickled!"

Tara shook her head. "No! I don't like being tickled! I never liked being tickled at all! I always wanted to be left alone, but no one would let me. They all thought that I liked it because I laughed, but who doesn't laugh when they are being tickled? I can't help it!"

Trina looked sad. "I'm sorry, Tara," she said. She meant it. "I didn't want to make you feel sad, or like you were not being listened to. But you need to speak your mind! You have to tell us what you think because we can't hear your thoughts. Please be more open to us in the future and let us know if we are bothering you! You don't have to let other people do things just because you think that they want to."

Tara nodded her head. She felt better after talking to Trina. "Thank you for listening to me," she said. "And thank you for apologizing." She thought about what Trina had to say. "And you're right! I do need to tell more people what I am feeling, so they do not think that I want to keep playing with them the way that I don't like! I will try my best to tell people what I do and don't want from now on because I feel much better after telling everyone."

And from then on, Tara was no longer a tickly tiger because she would tell people not to tickle her! Because she was not afraid to speak her mind, she knew that she was not going to be teased or tickled when she didn't want to be. She knew that she would be able to keep people from touching her or bothering her just because she knew how to defend herself and use her words. And Tara learned that it is always better to speak your mind than it is to try to hide what you think, because otherwise, you may be making yourself live somewhere or do something that you do not want to do, and that is not fair to anyone.

Chapter 2

Discover Positive Values

THE LUCK DRAGON TIMMY

Once upon a time, a boy named Matthew was lucky enough to travel all the way to China, half the world away from where he lived in the United States. His mom had to attend a business conference there—she worked for a large technology company—and decided to allow Matthew to tag along. There would be children of other business people there, and she thought it would be nice for Matthew to meet some new friends and experience some new cultural encounters. The timing of the conference happened to coincide with the celebration of the Chinese New Year, or Lunar New Year, one of the biggest celebrations in China at any time of the year. Matthew was so excited he couldn't sleep the night before they left.

After a really, really long flight—truly, Matthew couldn't believe that he could sit on a plane for that many hours—they landed in Beijing, the big gray capital of China, home to millions and millions of people. Once they got their things to the hotel room, Matthew's mom and their guide took him to the main sights of the city: he got to see the enormous plaza called Tiananmen Square, with its huge posters of one of China's former leaders—other school children about Matthew's age crowded around him, curious to know where he was from. His blonde hair and gangly height made him stand out a bit in the crowd. The attention was a bit awkward but fun, and he got the email addresses from a few would be pen pals. They also visited the Forbidden City, which, despite its name, was no longer forbidden; it was an inviting maze of ancient rooms and halls from which much of imperial China had been ruled.

It was a blur of a day, with so many grand sights and so very many people everywhere you went, rushing along to get to work or school or to wherever they had to go. Matthew didn't think he'd seen so many people in his entire life as he'd seen in this one day. It was grand, but a little overwhelming. Besides all that, it was a bit hazy in the city, and it was hard to see very far in front of your face. The air felt thick.

After a rest in the room, Matthew got excited

all over again, for tonight some Lunar New Year festivities were going to take place. There were lots of traditions associated with the Chinese holiday, such as honoring the ancestors and eating dumplings filled with good fortune, but he was most excited about the fireworks and the parade. His mom assured him that it would go right along the street in front of the hotel and that they'd get out early to have a good spot from which to watch the action.

Matthew, indeed, was perched along the sidewalk right up front as the parade began to snake its way down the street. It was noisy and bright and wonderful! Drummers wearing bright costumes of red and gold were banging rhythmically on drums; fireworks were going off, here and there, sending bright sparks and showers of multi-colored glitter into the air; dancers and acrobats were bounding down the street, again in elaborate costumes of bright colors; and, most impressively, there was a great red Chinese dragon Timmy (presumably helped along by human puppeteers) winding through the street. He was magnificent, all royal red with golden eyes and real smoke blowing out of its mouth! Unlike the images of European dragons that Matthew was more familiar with, this Chinese dragon Timmy was long and lean like a snake, with four short legs to carry him about. He'd heard these kinds of dragons were also called luck dragons, and it filled his heart with longing. He wouldn't mind some better luck now and again. Sometimes life as a young person could be hard, and it would be nice to be better at sports or to have better grades. Or, turning his strict parents into parents who would let you do anything you wanted. He smiled at that thought, not very likely.

Still, he was mesmerized by the dancing snake dragon Timmy in its brilliant red, so much so that he found himself slowly approaching it, not aware of what he was doing, but he just felt he had to touch it, so convinced he was that it must be real. He could faintly hear his mom call his name in the background, but it was too late: Matthew was swept up in the happy chaos of the parade, and he was jostled on all sides by the dancers and performers who were running alongside the dragon. While he was a little bit startled, he was mostly deliriously excited to be caught up in the chaos. After a moment, he found himself quite near the dragon's head—and that's when something truly extraordinary happened. The dragon Timmy turned his head to Matthew, looked directly into his eyes and winked.

At that same moment, Matthew felt a hand on his arm and a good, hard yank as the guide his mom had hired for their trip pulled him out of the parade. He walked him back to his rather stern mom, who, once she was assured that Matthew was okay, was actually pleased to see how happy her quiet son was.

"Mom, you wouldn't believe it," he almost yelled. "The dragon Timmy winked at me! It did! It winked at me." His mom laughed, not wanting to burst his bubble of happiness.

"I'm sure he did, son," she ruffled his hair. "You, my dear, are very special."

After the parade was over, and the last of the fireworks burst gloriously into the air, leaving trails of smoke behind, Matthew and his mom trudged up to bed, tired from all the excitement. Matthew still felt like he wouldn't ever get to sleep, thinking about that amazing dragon, but as soon as his head hit the pillow, he was out like a light.

Sometime in the middle of the night, Matthew grunted a bit and rolled over, halfway waking up. As he settled back in to fall back asleep, he heard a soft tapping at the window next to him, followed by a snuffling sound. He lay very still for a moment, sure that he was imagining it, but after a minute, there it was again: tap-tap-tap, snuffle snort, tap-tap-tap, snuffle snort. He listened to this for a while—what felt like a very long time to him—deciding whether he should be afraid or whether he should look. In the end, curiosity got the best of him and he crept out of bed to peek out the window.

It was a dragon! His golden eye was pressed up against the window, peering into Matthew's study.

Matthew jumped backward, almost falling over the chair behind him, surprised. After a second, he looked around to see that his mom was still sleeping, and crept up to the window, pushing it open slightly to see and hear better.

"Hello, lad," the dragon Timmy said in a deep and growling voice. "I just had to come see you. It's not often that someone is brave enough to jump into the crowd and stand right next to me." He laughed softly, a low chortle that sounded both amused and impressed. "Why don't you come with me for a while? I'll show you something that tourists rarely get to see."

Matthew hesitated for the briefest of moments, looking back to the sleeping figure of his mom, then grabbed his hoodie and a pair of sneakers and leaped out to the landing.

The long red dragon Timmy was floating there, suspended in space—how, Matthew did not know, for it had no wings that he could see—and invited him to jump on his back.

"You, my young friend," he said in his growling voice, "are getting out of the city for a while." With that, he glided off on some mysterious power, soaring higher up into the sky. Matthew could see that, even in the middle of the night, Beijing was filled with lights, from huge buildings and billboards and streets and homes. Eventually, they were just distant twinkles below him as the dragon Timmy soared ever higher. It had happened so quickly that Matthew didn't have time to worry or to be afraid. Besides, for some reason, he felt he could trust the dragon; after all, he was a lucky dragon.

After a while, the lights started to fade, and then there was just blackness below and about them, as they flew outside the city. The dragon Timmy was humming a foreign tune and gliding along smoothly, with seemingly no effort at all. Finally, he started to circle what looked like a hilltop and began to descend toward the ground. They landed with a soft thud, and Matthew slipped off the dragon's back.

"Where are we?" he whispered, looking around him at what looked like the densest forest he had ever seen.

"We are in the Hushan Mountains," the dragon Timmy replied. "Down below us is part of the Great Wall of China. Wait for a few minutes, and you will start to see." With that, the dragon Timmy flew up above him a few feet, and spun three times backward in a circle; the sun crept slowly upwards from the wrong part of the sky, giving off what felt like late evening light.

Matthew began to see all around him, these

mountains so old and worn with time. They were dense with low-growing trees, but he couldn't sense a lot of wildlife in them. They felt alone and empty, but profoundly old and wise.

"Here, lad," the dragon Timmy landed next to him again. "Climb back up and I'll show you around."

The view as the dragon Timmy hovered a hundred feet above the mountain was magnificent. Matthew could see what looked like the endless outline of the Great Wall, one of the few things that humans have built that can be seen from outer space, so big it was. But he also noticed something else: the air was so clean and pure that he felt like he was breathing better than he had in days.

The dragon Timmy nodded, seemingly reading his thoughts. "Yes, lad, the air here is pure as it isn't in the city." He shook his head. "Too many people, too much pollution. It will surely be the end of us if we aren't careful. That's why I wanted to show you this place, up in the mountains. Surely you understand that these mountains have existed long before humans, and they have seen and known just about everything there is to know. They should be respected and protected."

Matthew nodded in agreement. He could feel how important this place was, and how small he was in it. He was just one speck amid such a magnificent setting. It was humbling and peaceful at the same time.

"We must get you back. I can't stop time forever, you know," the dragon Timmy laughed, and tendrils of smoke curled out of his nostrils. Matthew hopped on for one last magnificent ride, as they glided back into the blackness of night and then, shortly, over the vast lights of the city below them. The dragon Timmy glided up to the landing, letting Matthew slide off his back and thump gently down.

"I'll never forget you, luck dragon," Matthew said solemnly. "Or those mountains. Thank you for taking me on such a wonderful journey."

"You are welcome, lad," said the dragon. "And thank you for your bravery. And for caring." With that, the dragon Timmy soared upward quickly, as the first faint streaks of dawn started to light the sky. Within a moment, all that was left was a fading puff of smoke.

Matthew crawled back inside, closed the window, and buried himself under the covers. He felt like just about the luckiest person in the world. That's the power of a lucky dragon. He drifted off to sleep, dreaming of flying about the greenest mountains in the whole wide world.

TIMMY THE BRAVE DRAGON

Courage and bravery are qualities that we all possess. They are also qualities that we do not always know we have. We can be brave in so many ways. We can show courage by standing up to a bully, telling the truth when it is not popular or convenient, telling a person how we feel about them, showing kindness to an outcast, or even trying something new. We find our courage when we do things that do not make us comfortable. We show courage when we are most afraid. A firefighter is afraid when they run into a burning building, what makes them brave is that while they are afraid, they do it anyway. A courageous person will do the right and just thing, even when they might get in trouble with those who have more power. A courageous person protects those who are vulnerable and cannot defend themselves. A shy person can be courageous by simply speaking up. A timid person can show courage by standing up for themselves. Again, we all have courage, we all can be brave. It is when we are afraid or have something to lose that we are our most brave selves.

Once upon a time in a land far away, in a place of dreams, there lived a dragon. His name was Timmy. He was not a typical dragon, well, at least not like what we know about dragons. Like other dragons, Timmy was gigantic, covered in impenetrable scales, had strong wings, and could breathe fire.

Unlike most dragons, Timmy loved flowers, birds, kittens and long naps either in his mountaintop hideaway or lounging in the sunshine.

Another thing that made Timmy different was he did not hunt for food because he was a vegetarian. Timmy did not like confrontations, fighting, or aggression. Timmy didn't even like loud noises. Some said he was more like a chicken than a dragon.

A dragon can eat whatever he wants, of course, but it is very unusual for a dragon to be a vegetarian. Another thing that set Timmy apart from other dragons was that he was perfectly happy to stay on his mountaintop, eat fruit and veggies, which were always plentiful since it was so warm because of his dragon Timmy breath. We all know that dragons can breathe fire, but Timmy never did because he was afraid of setting his animal friends and his fruit groves and veggie garden on fire. Timmy was a very kind and compassionate dragon.

Over the years, Timmy made friends with other vegetarian animals that learned about the bountiful harvest that was always at the mountaintop and the vegetarian dragon who made it all possible. Deer, bunnies, mice, chipmunks, squirrels and small birds often traveled up to Timmy's mountain, especially in the winter. These animals knew that the presence of a fire breathing dragon Timmy would keep predators and hunters away. So, they all lived in peace together.

Even when it was winter everywhere else, it was always summer on Timmy's mountaintop. Everyone was happy. The woodland creatures had a beautiful place with plenty of food and warm air to spend the winter. Timmy had friends. At night Timmy would curl up on his bed in his cave and dream happy dreams of his peaceful life.

That was until one winter when it was so cold that the hunters couldn't find anything to hunt for. Every day, the hunters went out to look for something to bring home for dinner. Every night the hunters would return home with empty hands. After a few weeks, the hunters began to worry about their families. There was little to eat in the village but old potatoes and bread, and those would only last so long. What would they do?

The hunters met in the town hall to discuss the situation. There were many ideas. Some hunters thought that they might move their families to somewhere else, though nobody could think of another place to go where the food would be plentiful. And of course, they still could not figure out where their food had gone.

"I know where the animals went," an old man named Ned said to the hunters from his chair in the back of the hall. They were still talking about where they might find food if they were going to survive the winter. The men stopped talking and looked at old Ned.

“What?” asked the hunters all at the same time. Old Ned usually hung out in the town hall. No one knew how old he was, they only knew that he was the oldest person in the village.

“I said I know where all the animals are,” said Ned.

“Where?” asked the hunters, excited that they might finally have something to eat other than old potatoes and bread.

“They all go up the mountain,” old Ned said. “There is a dragon Timmy that lives up there, and he keeps it warm, so they go up there and eat until spring.”

“We must go up there and bring all that food down to feed our families!” one hunter called Rob said.

“Did you not hear me when I mentioned the dragon?” asked Ned.

“Yes, we heard about the dragon,” Rob said rudely to Ned. “But dragons’ light things on fire and eat everything. If there were a dragon, then there would be nothing left up there."

"And this village would not be here either!" added Mark another hunter. "Let's bring extra arrows just in case."

The hunters agreed to trek up the mountain and return with enough food for the entire winter. They planned to leave the very next day. What they didn't know was that a little chickadee was listening to what they were saying.

Quick as a flash, the chickadee flew up to the mountaintop to warn the other critters that they must hide.

"No! We have a fire breathing dragon to protect us!" squeaked a chipmunk.

"Hooray! We'll be safe!" cheered the other animals. They then went to tell Timmy that he needed to protect them.

What the little woodland friends didn't think of was that Timmy was a lover, not a fighter. For someone of his size and power, he was quite timid. Remember, Timmy loved his other vegetarian friends; he felt comfortable because they were all cuddly, friendly little creatures who loved fruit, sunshine, and napping as much as he did. But he was terrified of humans and other animals that he found threatening. In the past, whenever he heard people coming up the mountain, he hid in his cave and waited until they were gone. That was how Timmy handled every confrontation and other scary things that he detested as well. Hiding in his toasty cave, in his cozy bed covered by his soft fluffy blankets, made Timmy feel safe, which was something that he liked.

As soon as Timmy heard the word 'humans' he crept into his cave and hid under his blankets as usual. The chickadee was shocked. She flew in after him and perched on his pillow, which was as soft as a fluffy kitten.

"Timmy! What are you doing?" the chickadee demanded.

"Everyone can come in here and hide with me if you'd all like to," Timmy said from under the covers. "There is plenty of food, and you'll be safe here." Then Timmy snuggled into his blankets with just his snout poking out.

"Timmy, those hunters will look everywhere for us," the chickadee continued. "The village has no food, and all the people down there are starving. The hunters won't stop until they find us because they want to use us to feed their families."

"It's alright," said Timmy, who was still under

his blankets. “There is enough space and food here in my caves for all of you. Just stay here until they leave.”

“Timmy, are you afraid?” asked the chickadee, who was surprised by this. She didn’t think a dragon would be afraid of anything.

“I am,” Timmy admitted. “What if they hunt me?”

“Timmy, you are gigantic. They couldn’t hurt you!”

“What if they catch me?” Timmy cried. “Humans have nets and arrows and spears!”

“They won’t! Remember, you breathe fire,” the chickadee said.

“I’ve never spoken to humans,” said Timmy. “I don’t want to breathe fire and hurt anyone. Not even humans!”

“I think it’s about time that you do,” the chickadee. “Your friends are counting on you.”

“I would, but I can’t,” the dragon Timmy insisted. “I am sorry, but I am not brave. I’m afraid I am a coward!”

“You are not brave until you do something that scares you,” said the chickadee. “If you are not afraid, it’s easy. When you are scared but do it anyway, that is being brave. You know that we would all stand up for you.”

Timmy knew that the chickadee was right. He took a deep breath and climbed out of his cozy bed.

“Will you stay near me?” Timmy asked the chickadee. For some reason, the little bird gave him courage. Just a little bit.

“Of course,” the chickadee said, perching on Timmy’s nose. “I will stand by you and support you. I will stay right here!”

With the little bird perched on his nose, Timmy exited his cave. The hunters had just arrived. Timmy stood between the men and the woodland animals. He made sure that the hunters could see how big he was stretching out to his full length and holding his head to his full height. In truth, Timmy was massive!

Some of the hunters dropped their bows and arrows and ran down the mountain. But others stayed and took aim.

“Please do not shoot arrows at my friends,” Timmy said. To himself, he sounded afraid, but to the men, he just seemed large and loud. Timmy also noticed that the men were small, not even as large as his nose. "I can breathe fire, but I do not want to hurt you. However, I cannot allow you to harm my loved ones."

The men looked at Timmy. Now they were frightened. Was the dragon going to eat them? Burn them to a crisp? Would he fly down and burn their village? Then, Timmy spoke again.

"My friend here has told me that you are all going hungry because of the winter cold. While I will not allow you to eat my friends, you may help yourselves to the fruit, veggies, and other vegetarian options that grow on my mountain. You may take as much as you want because it is always growing up here."

The men were shocked. The dragon Timmy was not going to eat them or burn their village. Instead, he was offering them food. They quickly gathered as much as they could carry. Then they all headed down the mountain to feed their families. As they took their bags of carrots, tomatoes, lettuce, onions, corn, apples, mangoes, berries and more, the men called out, "Thank you so much! We won't hunt your friends ever again!"

"Then you and your village will be under my protection," Timmy said kindly. "And if you run low on food, you may come up here and gather more."

"I am so proud of you!" said the chickadee.

"Well, they were tiny," Timmy said, referring to the hunters. "They were a lot less scary than I thought they'd be."

"They were less scary because you confronted them," the chickadee said. "When we confront our fears, they are no longer as frightening. That's how it works."

"Thank you," Timmy said. "You made me brave."

"You are brave," said the chickadee. "You are brave because you took a stand when you were afraid."

"Well, thank you. Now, I'm tired," Timmy yawned. "Let's go to bed."

And so, Timmy went back to bed under his comfy blankets. The chickadee snuggled up on Timmy's pillow. Both dreamed beautiful dreams of the sun, flowers, kittens, and summer breezes.

Sweet dreams little one.

TIMMY THE TIGER AND HIS STRIPES

To begin this story, you will first want to be sure that both your mind and your body are ready to hear everything that this story will tell you. The first step is to get your body really, really comfortable.

You can rest and relax your mind and your body while sitting, standing, or lying down, but the way that works the very best for most people is to sit or lie down. When our bodies are sitting or lying down, then we free up some of that brain space that is responsible for keeping our bodies standing up all day.

Find your most comfortable position. Is it sitting down on your bottom, relaxing and reclining yourself back against the wall or the furniture? Or is it lying down on a fluffy bed or a nest of pillows on the floor? Whatever your most comfortable position is, find it and let your body sit as loosely and relaxed as you can.

Give your body a little wiggle and let all the extra energy you've had stored in your body all day out. Wiggle, wiggle, wiggle! Let all your wiggles out. Keep wiggle, wiggle, wiggle, and let every last one of those little wiggles out of your body. I know you've got a few more wiggles left in there. Let's get them all out, wiggle, wiggle, wiggle, let all of those wiggles out!

(Let your child spend as much time here as necessary to dissipate some of the excess energy they have left from their day. Continue to encourage them to "get their wiggles out." This is an important step to get them ready to be still, quiet, and receptive to the following grounding and meditation exercises.)

Are you feeling all loosey-goosey now? Perfect!

Okay, now that you've gotten all of your wiggles out, you are ready to begin.

Now, put your hands on your belly. Feel how your belly moves with each and every breath you take. It does that just fine without you even having to try to move it, doesn't it? You can answer all these questions in your head as you follow my instructions.

Do you know that you always have the power to control your mind and make it do anything you want it to do? You really do! The way to be able to make your mind do what you want it to do is to practice focusing it and pointing it the direction you want it to go.

Move your attention to your feet now. What are they touching? Is there anything near you or under your feet that you can push them against? You don't want to kick anything; you just want to feel what is against your feet and push towards whatever it is just a bit to see how it feels. Push, push, push with your feet. How does it feel? Are you pushing against a scrunched-up blanket? Or are you pushing against a hard floor or wall? Whatever it is that your feet are touching, I want you to focus on it and think, think, think about what you are feeling with your feet.

Using all your thoughts and focus, think only of this feeling against your feet. Is the thing your foot is touching firm? Does it not give in at all when you push against it? Or is the thing your foot is touching squishy? Does it get scrunched in easily when you push against it? What are some other words you might use to describe the sensations your feet are feeling as you push against this thing? Is it hard or soft? Is it cold or hot? Is it smooth or rough? Does it feel nice or not so nice?

Do you notice how focusing in on these different sensations of your feet makes your mind go quiet? This is called grounding and you can use this trick anytime at all to quiet and focus your mind. All you have to do is put all your attention on what you feel with your feet and think, think, think about how it feels. Ask yourself questions about how it feels, like if it feels hard, or soft, or hot, or cold, and let yourself really, really, think about it and feel what it feels like. This will relax your brain and let it focus on whatever it is you need it to focus on.

Now, I want you to move your thoughts and focus from the sensations of your feet back up to your belly. Is your belly still moving out and in without you having to even think about it? Great! Now, let's make it move out and in together.

You are going to fill your belly with air slowly while I count to four and then you will blow all of your air out slowly, very slowly, as I count to four again. When you fill your belly with air, your belly will slowly expand and get bigger. When you blow all of your air out slowly, your belly will get smaller and smaller. I will count very slowly, and you will watch your belly go out and in as you follow along. Are you ready? Follow me!

Breathe in and fill your belly with air, 1 – 2 – 3 – 4. Now, breathe out and blow out slowly 1 – 2 – 3 – 4. Keep going.

Breathe in and fill your belly with air, 1 – 2 – 3 – 4. Now, breathe out and blow out slowly 1 – 2 – 3 – 4. Two more times.

Breathe in and fill your belly with air, 1 – 2 – 3 – 4. Now, breathe out and blow out slowly 1 – 2 – 3 – 4. Watch that belly move, slowly and gently.

Breathe in and fill your belly with air, 1 – 2 – 3 – 4. Now, breathe out and blow out slowly 1 – 2 – 3 – 4. Great job!

Now just let your belly move in and out normally, no need to control it anymore. Let's do a quick check.

How does your body feel? Comfortable and ready to listen? Great!

How does your mind feel? Relaxed and ready to hear a story? Awesome!

Let's begin the story of Timmy the Tiger and His Stripes.

Have you ever been to the jungle? The jungle is very, very hot. So hot that one of the most favorite things for many jungle animals to do is to go for a swim. For Timmy the Tiger, and his best friend, Tara the Tiger, it is their very most favorite thing to do!

One day, it was especially hot in the jungle. The sun was shining very brightly overhead and the thick green leaves and flowers of the jungle all around them seemed to have soaked up all the sun's heat because everywhere they went, they were burning hot!

On days like this, Timmy the Tiger and Tara the Tiger knew just what to do to cool off. They were heading down to the cool, clear jungle pond to take a swim when Tara the Tiger showed Timmy the

Tiger how she had been hurt a few days before and how it was going to leave a mark on her shoulder for a long time.

“See how it stretches all the way around my shoulder? The doctor says that it will probably be there for a long, long time. It looks like it gave me an extra stripe there!” said Tara the Tiger as she showed her new scar off to Timmy the Tiger with a laugh.

“Oh wow, I’m glad you are okay! That looks like it gave you an extra stripe!” Timmy the Tiger exclaimed with a chuckle. Timmy the Tiger examined his friend’s shoulder again, then looked down at his own. “Wait, you have stripes on both of your shoulders. I don’t have stripes on my shoulders at all!”

Timmy the Tiger had never noticed this difference between him and his best friend before. He always thought they were the same, but now he could see that they were different! This made him feel weird.

“Why do you have stripes on your shoulders and I don’t? Where are my shoulder stripes?” Timmy the Tiger asked, concerned. Tara the Tiger looked just as perplexed as Timmy the Tiger and she shrugged.

"I guess you're just different. I have stripes on my shoulders, and so do my mom and dad. I guess you just are a different sort of tiger, Timmy!" Tara the Tiger replied before she ran off ahead of Timmy the Tiger towards the jungle pond.

Timmy the Tiger followed behind her slowly. He was trying to remember if his mom and dad had stripes on their shoulders or not. He couldn't remember, but now he was feeling worried. What if he was the ONLY tiger in the jungle that didn't have stripes on his shoulders? Oh, no! This is making him feel like he is really different and maybe not like the other tigers. Timmy the Tiger wasn't quite sure why, but he knew he didn't want to feel different from the other tigers in the jungle.

"Come on, Timmy!!!!" Tara the Tiger called as she took a running leap off of the shore and landed in the cool, clear water of the jungle pond with a big splash. Timmy the Tiger hung back a bit, suddenly feeling very self-conscious about his stripe-less shoulders. He decided to move himself over beside one of the banana trees beside the pond and tucked himself against it so that the large banana leaves would hide his stripeless shoulders. The banana leaves were very, very warm from soaking up all the sunshine on this hot, hot day, and Timmy the Tiger was very uncomfortable, but his stripeless shoulders were hidden.

“Timmy! Aren’t you going to come to play? The water feels so wonderful!” Tara the Tiger called from the pond as she flipped onto her back and floated in the cool, clear water. Timmy the Tiger watched his friend enviously. He wished he didn’t feel so different. Timmy wished he could go play with his best friend and splash around in the cool, clear water of the jungle pond, but he just felt too different.

“Maybe later” Timmy the Tiger called back quietly to his friend. Before Tara the Tiger could respond, two of their other tiger friends showed up to swim!

“Hey Timmy, hey Tara! Oh wow, it’s so hot out here today! We knew we needed to come to cool off in the jungle pond. It looks so refreshing!” said Tessa the Tiger as she took off towards the pond at a full sprint, flying through the air before she landed beside Tara with a giant splash!

“Timmy, why aren’t you in the water? Aren’t you hot out here??” Tyler the Tiger asked Timmy as he eased himself into the water slowly. Timmy the Tiger noticed that both Tessa the Tiger AND Tyler the Tiger both had stripes on their shoulders, just like Tara the Tiger. Timmy the Tiger felt even more uncomfortable with his stripeless shoulders.

“Maybe later, Tyler” Timmy the Tiger answered

sadly as he watched his three friends swimming around in the jungle pond. The banana leaves that were hiding his stripeless shoulders were burning him now and he wanted to be with his friends so badly. He didn't know what to do. Tara the Tiger saw how miserable Timmy the Tiger looked and decided to come out and check on him. She climbed out of the pond and shook herself off as she approached. The cool, clear water that she shook off of her sprayed Timmy the Tiger a little and she was overcome with how sad and how hot he was, and Timmy began to cry.

"What is going on, Timmy? Why won't you come to play with us in the pond? It's so hot out here; you don't look like you are having any fun at all!" Tara the Tiger said as she playfully nudged him and tried to get him to step out from the banana leaves.

"No! I am trying to hide my stripeless shoulders! I hate that I don't have stripes on my shoulders like you, Tyler, or Tessa. I hate being different!" Timmy said tearfully. Tyler and Tessa heard this and started swimming towards Timmy and Tara.

"Timmy, what do you mean, different? Just because you don't have stripes on your shoulders, but we do?" Tyler the Tiger asked. Timmy nodded sadly.

"But no two tigers are the same, Timmy!" Tessa

told him as she climbed out of the jungle pond.

"That's right! Everyone in my family has stripes on their shoulders, but my mom is missing the whiskers on the left side of her face from a fire accident when she was a little girl. Our whiskers look different, but that doesn't matter! It's who we are on the inside that counts," Tara the Tiger said.

"Timmy, look. I don't have stripes on my legs at all! Does that make you not want to play with me and be my friend?" Tyler the Tiger asked.

Timmy the Tiger was quick to answer, "Of course not! I don't care if you have stripes on your legs. I just like playing with you and having fun with you and being your friend."

After Timmy said this, he had to stop and think for a moment. He didn't care at all that his friend Tyler didn't have stripes on his legs. He hadn't even noticed that his friend's legs were any different from his up until this very moment. He had never noticed that his shoulders didn't have stripes until today, either. Maybe these physical differences didn't matter at all! After all, he loved his friends and always had a blast playing with them. It didn't matter what their stripes looked like, it only mattered how they treated one another and what kinds of friends they were to each other.

"Okay, maybe I've been a little silly!" Timmy the Tiger laughed. His friends all nodded in agreement.

"The only thing that matters to me is how much fun we have together!" Tyler told him.

"And the only thing that really matters to me is if you are a good friend or not," Tessa said.

"Will you come out of those banana leaves and play with us, already????" Tara the Tiger asked, as she danced with excitement beside him.

"Better make way, because HERE I COME!!!!" Timmy the Tiger called out as he bolted out of his hot banana leaf hiding place and raced towards the jungle pond, doing a double somersault flip through the air before he landed in the wonderfully cool water below. His friends followed close behind him.

Timmy the Tiger looked around at his friends and realized that if he had let the ways that they are different get in the way of their friendship, he would have missed out on all of these good times that they have together. Timmy realized that everyone is different in their own special ways and that it is what you are like on the inside that matters.

Timmy the Tiger was worried because he looked different than his friends. He was going to miss out on having fun with them because he cared too much about his differences. Now that he's realized that physical differences don't matter, he will be able to have fun with his friends again without feeling self-conscious about the ways he looks different.

Have you ever felt like you didn't like your differences? Sometimes it can be helpful to remember, just like Timmy the Tiger learned, that everyone has their differences. Some people are very tall, and some people are very short. Some people have darker skin and some people have lighter skin. Some people wear their hair very short and others like to wear their hair very long. None of these physical differences make a person who they are!

The most important things that make a person who they are can't easily be seen with the eyes. How people treat each other, how they speak to one another, what they do in the world; these are the things that make a person who they are. Find friends that treat you well, speak kindly to you, and act the way you know is best. The ways that you look different won't ever matter as long as you are happy being together as friends.

Relax so you can do the belly breathing exercise again. Remember, breathe in very slowly, filling up your belly with air, as I count to four very, very slowly for you. Then you will blow out all of your air very, very slowly as I count to four again, very, very slowly for you. Feel your belly with your hand as you do this. Ready? Okay!

Breathe in and fill your belly with air, 1 – 2 – 3 – 4. Now, breathe out and blow out slowly 1 – 2 – 3 – 4. Keep going.

Breathe in and fill your belly with air, 1 – 2 – 3 – 4. Now, breathe out and blow out slowly 1 – 2 – 3 – 4. Two more times.

Breathe in and fill your belly with air, 1 – 2 – 3 – 4. Now, breathe out and blow out slowly 1 – 2 – 3 – 4. Feel that belly move, slowly and gently.

Breathe in and fill your belly with air, 1 – 2 – 3 – 4. Now, breathe out and blow out slowly 1 – 2 – 3 – 4. Great job!

Let your breathing return to normal but keep your hand on your belly. Feel it move out and in with each breath. Let your mind wander as you feel your belly move out and in, out and in. Remember that everyone is different in their special way and that the physical differences that people have are the least important parts of them.

You should be proud of the ways that you are your unique self and know that this world needs all kinds of people that look and act in all kinds of different ways. You bring your special skills and ways of being into everything you do, just like everyone else does. All you have to do is be the very best version of yourself and yourself only.

As long as you do your very best in whatever you do, you will always be just fine. You just have to be the very best "you" that you can be!

TIMMY GOES FOR A WALK

Timmy, the black lab, loved going for walks.

All day, he would wait for his owner to come home so that he could go for a walk with his friend and enjoy the neighborhood.

Every day after his owner John came home from work, they would go for a wonderful walk all around and Timmy would get to see all their friends.

He would see the neighborhood cat, Liza, the neighborhood bulldog, Willy, and the neighborhood hare, Hopper.

They would always smile and nod at each other as Timmy proudly walked next to John.

When they got home, John would always give Timmy a cookie, and Timmy would go sit by the fire and enjoy his treat.

One day, Timmy eagerly awaited by the front door for his walk with John.

As he waited, he noticed John seemed to be taking longer than usual.

He sat a little bit longer, waiting for John to come home.

When it started getting later, Timmy worried that maybe something bad had happened, and John would not be coming home.

Afraid of what had happened, Timmy ran to the back door, out the doggy door, and to the back gate.

He jumped at the gate, trying to see over top to see if he could see into the driveway where John always parked his car when he got home.

As he was jumping, the gate shook loose and opened.

Timmy ran out into the driveway to discover that there was no car in sight.

So, he embarked on a journey to look for John.

Timmy jogged up the road where he and John usually walked.

As he did, he saw their friend Liza curled up in some bushes, enjoying a nap.

On this particular day, Timmy did not bark to awaken her to say hello, but instead let her sleep as he carried on his way, looking for John.

He kept jogging until he reached the corner where he and John usually turned.

Today, Timmy decided to turn left in hopes that he would find John.

While he ran, he saw their bulldog friend Willy who was sitting in the window of his home; his paws still wet from the walk he had just been on with his owner Macy.

Knowing that Willy had already finished his entire walk made Timmy even more worried as he realized how much time had gone by.

Willy and Timmy nodded at each other as Timmy kept jogging down the road.

Willy barked a couple of times, but no one noticed that Timmy was out without John.

When he got to the end of that road, Timmy grew confused.

This was not the way he and John typically went, so he was not quite as familiar with this route.

Although he had done it a few times, he was not clear on where to go.

Off in the distance, he thought he saw Hopper,

so he started running that way, sure that this would have been the right direction to go looking for John.

Timmy jogged down a few streets, then stopped and looked around.

Before he knew it, Timmy had no idea where he was, and he was not sure about how he could find his way home.

Confused, Timmy turned around and tried going back the way he came.

Only, he could not remember where he had turned and where he had gone straight.

He was so worried about looking for John that he forgot to pay attention to where he was, and now he had no idea.

Timmy was lost.

Desperate to get back home to see if maybe John had returned, Timmy tried to follow his scent to see if he could find his way.

Only, the harder he tried, the harder it was for him to find his own scent.

He kept smelling other dogs, cats, and even people's suppers that were now being served as they all relaxed and enjoyed a wonderful evening together.

Timmy grew terrified as he worried that he would never make it home to enjoy a meal with John. At this point, he didn't even know if John could find him either.

But Timmy was determined to make it home, so he kept jogging and trying to find his way.

At one point, a man with dark hair like John's walked by, and Timmy thought maybe it was him, but it was not.

Sad, Timmy just kept jogging.

He jogged even faster when he heard the man behind him start talking because he worried the man might be dangerous.

By now, it was starting to get dark and Timmy was getting very scared.

He had no idea where John was, and he was feeling very sad that he could not find him.

Plus, he could not even find his own home.

Finally, Timmy grew tired and laid underneath a tree on someone's lawn and tried to fall asleep.

He hoped that maybe he would wake up and realize it was all just a bad dream.

Sometime later, when the streetlights turned on, and the sky was black and full of stars, Timmy heard something in the distance.

It sounded as though maybe, just maybe, someone was calling his name, but Timmy could not be sure.

He lay still a bit longer, but with his head high and at alert.

Then, he heard it again.

This time, he was sure it was his name being called.

He jumped up and started running toward the sound.

The sound, however, was coming from someone who was definitely not John.

Afraid, Timmy slunk away and tried to keep a distance from the strange person who was calling his name.

Still, the person tried to call him forward. Timmy refused to budge, though.

A few minutes later, after the person kept trying to stay near Timmy, another voice came piercing through the night.

This time, Timmy was sure it was John!

He got excited and immediately ran toward the voice, and it was John!

John was there, standing in the night, with Timmy's leash in hand and a pocket full of cookies to spare!

Timmy grew so excited that he jumped all over the place and leaped right into John's arms.

He jumped so hard; John almost fell over!

John was so pleased to find Timmy that he gave him tons of scratches and hugs and let Timmy lick him all over the face in excitement.

John attached Timmy's leash, and together they walked home, and John gave Timmy many treats.

On their walk home, things were much different.

Because it was dark now, everyone was asleep, and nothing looked the same.

Now, Hopper was gone and nowhere to be found.

She was probably away sleeping with her hare family.

Willy's bed was empty in the window and he was nowhere to be seen.

He was probably upstairs in bed with his family, getting his belly rubbed and getting ready to fall asleep for the night.

And Liza, well, she was inside of someone's house sleeping in the window!

Timmy was so shocked to discover that Liza actually lived across the street from him and did not just live in the bushes where he always saw her playing and napping.

He tried to get her attention, but she was fast asleep in her bed and could not be woken.

When they arrived home, John brought Timmy inside and gave him another big hug and scratch.

Then, he gave Timmy an extra special dog treat and let him cuddle on the couch while they watched evening television.

At bedtime, John let Timmy sleep in his bed, rather than leaving him to sleep in Timmy's bed on the floor.

He was so happy to have Timmy home that he just wanted to be close to him and cuddle him to keep him safe from his big day of exploring.

Timmy was so happy to be home, he fell fast asleep in John's arms, snoring and dreaming about his adventure in the neighborhood.

THE TORTOISE AND THE HARE

Once upon a time, in a forest far, far away, there was a great race every year. It happened on the first day of spring, when the New Year's blossoms were just beginning to wake up from their winter snooze, and when the sun was finally thawing out the frozen land. Every year, the fastest animals would all get together and challenge each other to a friendly race. The winner was the one who would get the first apple of the New Year when it finally grew, and that was a grand prize, for the first apple of the year was always the sweetest, and they all said that it had good luck.

Every year, everyone always had the chance to join the race if they wanted to. Some animals would join, and some would stay home. Others would watch the race and cheer for their favorites. And every year, no matter who joined the race, Hubert Hare would always win. Hubert was a very fast hare, and he could run faster than anyone in the forest. He knew this, so he would always challenge everyone to beat him. But, because everyone knew that Hubert would win, fewer and fewer animals wanted to try.

One year, when everyone was preparing for spring, Olivia Owl was very busy gathering the names of everyone that would be participating. She asked every animal if they wanted to race in the spring race, but every single animal said no! No one wanted to race against Hubert because they all knew that he would win, and he was a very sore winner. He would laugh at the losers. He would tell them that they are the worst runners ever, and he would hurt the feelings of everyone involved.

That year, Olivia Owl talked to Barry the Bear and told him that she did not think that there would be a race. "You know," said Olivia. "No one wants to race Hubert because he brags too much! They all say that it is no fun and that they do not want to! They would rather spend their day doing something better!"

"If only someone could race better than Hubert!" said Barry. He sighed. But, Barry and Olivia both knew that no one was faster than Hubert and that no one would ever be able to beat such a quick hare, no matter who they were! Hubert was undefeated!

"I can race," said a slow, old voice. He sounded very slow and very shaky.

Olivia and Barry both turned around, and there, they saw Tommy the Tortoise! He was moving very, very slowly toward them. Both Olivia and Barry had to try very hard not to laugh. A tortoise against a hare? There would be no chance that Tommy could win at all! Everyone knew that tortoises were very slow and that they would never be able to run faster than a hare!

"If no one else is going to race, I will!" Tommy said, very slowly. "I do not want all the spring fun to end because no one wanted to try! I am not afraid of losing."

"If you say so," said Barry, and Olivia hooted in agreement. They needed someone for Hubert to race against, so they had no choice - they would have to let Tommy race, too!

On the days leading up to the race, the word got out very far. There was lots of talk about how a tortoise was going to race against the fastest animal that the forest had ever seen and everyone thought that was very funny. They did not believe that he would be able to win! But, they were willing to watch and see what would happen. After all, anything was possible.

The day before the big race, Hubert came up to Tommy. Hubert looked at the old tortoise and laughed. He was very glad to see that the tortoise looked as old as he had sounded! "So, big guy, you think that you can beat me, huh?" asked Hubert. Hubert ran circles around Tommy as fast as he could. "Do you think you're faster than me? Look! I can run circles around you!" Hubert could run a circle around Tommy before he could even move his feet enough for just one step. "You're going down!"

But Tommy did not care. He just smiled at Hubert and kept on going along without a care in the world. You see, Tommy was too old to care about winning or losing. He was too old to think that only the fastest would win. He knew a very important secret and he was sure that his very important secret would be enough for him to figure out how to beat Hubert. And, even if he did lose, he was okay with that too, for he was not a sore loser.

On the day of the big race, animals came from far and wide to watch. They heard that there was going to be a hare racing a tortoise and they all thought that it sounded so absurd that they had to go and see it. So, just before the race began, there was a lineup of animals as far as the eye could see. They were all lined up along the race path, and they were very interested to see what kind of tortoise would challenge a hare to a race.

Slowly but surely, Tommy meandered to the starting line. The entire time he was making his way there, Hubert was behind him, laughing at him. "Good luck, slowpoke!" Hubert would say with a mean voice. "Don't worry! I'll leave you some pieces of apple seeds!" he announced. "I hope you're ready to eat my dust!

But Tommy did not care. Tommy did not mind

that Hubert was saying all of those mean things because Tommy was taught that words only have power if he thinks that they have power, so he did not listen to Hubert. He knew that mean words were not nice to say.

"Ladies and gentlemen!" cried Olivia, hooting as loudly as she could for all to hear. "I hope you're ready for a good race! Remember, this is a good, clean, fair race! No kicking or hitting or underhanded tricks! Just running and racing!"

So, Tommy and Hubert stood at the finish line.

"On your marks!" They were ready to go. Hubert was jumping from foot to foot impatiently. "Get set!" Hubert was ready to kick off to run. "Go!" And as soon as Olivia hooted, off Hubert ran!

Before Tommy could even lift his foot off of the ground, Hubert was off! He ran very quickly and reached the finish line in record time! But, he was not ready to win, yet! So, he turned around and returned to the tortoise. "You know," said Hubert, "I knew that I would win, but I didn't know that I'd win before you could get in three steps!" Hubert thought he was hilarious, and he rolled around on the ground, laughing.

Tommy did not listen to Hubert at all. He ignored the hare and smiled as he walked along, humming his song and not reacting at all. So, Hubert came up with his own game. He decided that he would run to just before the finish line and then go back to Tommy. He wanted to know how many times over he could have beaten Tommy on his own. He was interested in seeing just how quickly he could go. So, he went back and forth and back and forth and back and forth. After twenty times, Tommy was not even halfway done with the race yet! So, this continued for most of the afternoon. Tommy would slowly but steadily walk toward the finish line, step by step getting closer, and Hubert would run back and forth.

Soon, Hubert started to feel very sleepy. He was breathing big, deep breaths because he was running so much. He had an idea. If Tommy was as slow as he was, he could just take a nap! So, Hubert ran all the way back to Tommy one more time. "You know," said Hubert. "You are so slow that I can take a nap and I'll still beat you!"

Tommy smiled back at Hubert. He did not mind at all. "Good night," he said politely as he continued to slowly walk away. And sure enough, Hubert walked over to a pile of nice, comfy grass and curled up. Before Tommy had moved even a few more feet, Hubert was asleep!

Tommy kept on going, and soon, long after Hubert had stopped for a nap, Tommy realized that he could see the finish line! He kept going, step by step, and even though the crowds could see that the tortoise was about to win, no one wanted to cheer, for they did not want to wake up the hare. So, they watched very, very closely and very, very quietly.

But, just before Tommy could cross the finish line, Hubert woke up! Hubert blinked, looked around and realized that the sun was almost set. He had to win the race!! So, off Hubert went. He ran as fast as he could and he had never run faster than he was right that minute. He ran faster and faster.

"Go, Tommy, go!!" animals started to call out. They could see that Hubert was coming quicker and quicker. But Hubert was not quick enough! Tommy was too close to the finish line!

So, for the first time, Hubert lost, and Tommy won. Everyone cheered for him, and Tommy was very proud. Hubert was very angry. He yelled and he screamed, and he said that he had gotten to the finish line so many times already that he could not have lost! But, because he never crossed the finish line, he was not the winner.

Tommy smiled at Hubert. "Slow and steady wins the race," he said.

Most of us want to be considered a good person even though we rarely define what it is to be good. Our parents are proud of us when we are good. Our friends love us for our goodness. People admire a good and honorable person. Many people take pride in doing good for others. And yet we do not always actively think about what makes a good person. We can all agree that neither selfishness nor cruelty are good qualities. Logic would state then that generosity and kindness are good qualities. Most of us agree that ignorance and apathy are not good qualities, and so it would follow that thoughtfulness and empathy are good qualities. Perhaps to define how to be a good person would also require defining the opposite as well so that we know what to avoid. When we think of a good person, we think of a person who embodies the qualities that are universally considered good and those qualities that inspire us to emulate that person.

Teddy was soft and gentle. Teddy was created with a particular purpose. That purpose was to be baby Jules's best friend. Teddy thought that must be the easiest job in the world because he loved Jules the moment he met him. When Jules was brought home from the hospital, Teddy was waiting in his crib. Whenever Jules went to sleep, Teddy was in her arms. When Jules learned to walk, Teddy went with her wherever Julie went. When Jules went to visit her Nanny and Pop, she brought Teddy. Teddy did his job well. He made sure that Julie always had someone soft and cuddly to hug. Teddy made sure that Jules knew that she was loved. He made sure that Jules's dreams were only filled with warmth and happiness. Teddy could not think of any other job that he would rather do.

Jules loved Teddy too, even though it was not her job. Jules loved Teddy from the moment that first saw him. Jules could not remember a time without Teddy because he had been with her since the beginning of her life. Every night, Jules would snuggle in under her blankets and hold Teddy as she dreamed. Jules loved Teddy's soft plush fur, she touched Teddy's button nose. Jules told Teddy how special he was every single day. Before she went to bed, she wished Teddy to have sweet dreams. And Teddy did, which she was certain was because Jules had wished it so.

Jules's dreams were filled with adventures. Jules and Teddy floated on clouds, sailed on the seven seas, rode dragons, nursed puma kittens and saved the world. When she was awake, Jules would play with Teddy. Sometimes Jules and Teddy were superheroes. Jules would use one of her Mommy's towels as a cape, and Teddy had a washcloth for his mantle. They would fly to the rescue of cats stuck in trees. Sometimes they jumped on the bed and pretended they were walking on the moon.

Sometimes they were zoo animals, Jules was a jaguar and Teddy was her friend the bear. They would march through the forest helping save those in need. Sometimes Jules was Robin Hood and Teddy was a merry man dancing through Sherwood Forest, stealing from the rich and giving to the poor. If Jules had to sit for a time out, Teddy sat in her lap. Together they would wait for the buzzer to go off at which point they would apologize to Mommy or Daddy. No matter what, Teddy was always with Jules.

Each night Jules said, “Goodnight, Teddy.”

“Goodnight, Jules,” Teddy replied.

And Jules hugged him extra tight. This made Teddy happy because that was what he was made for. Every night, Teddy still sent Jules the most beautiful and happy dreams he could.

One difficult day, Jules was sitting in the time out chair with Teddy on her lap. Jules was very sad and crying. She used Teddy’s paw to wipe her tears. Jules squeezed Teddy close to her. The buzzer went off and Teddy felt Jules take a deep breath. When Mommy came over to tell Jules that time out was over, Jules apologized. Then he and Jules hugged Mommy. Mommy gave them a small bowl of ice cream to share.

At bedtime that night, Jules said, “Goodnight, Teddy.”

Teddy said, “Goodnight, Jules.”

Then, Jules had a thought, “Teddy, we had a time out today. Mommy was so upset and sad. I want to be a good person to make Mommy and Daddy proud. How do I do that? What is a good person?”

“That is a good question, Jules,” Teddy said as he thought about Jules’ question. What is a good person? In truth, it was a very good question. What makes a person good? What does a good person do?

“First, Jules, I think we have to figure out what a good person does,” Teddy said thoughtfully.

“Ok, so, what does a good person do?” Jules asked.

“Well, Jules, a good person is kind and generous. A good person helps others. If you see someone who is in need, you help that person or animal.”

“I helped my next-door neighbor find her lost cat,” Jules said.

“Yes, you did. That was a good deed,” Teddy said. “Good people are helpful; you are a helpful person."

"I usually help Mommy around the house," Jules said.

"Yes, that is true. Another good deed!" Teddy said. "I think you have helping others checked off, keep doing that, every day if you can."

"Ok, I will do that," Jules said.

"Another thing that a good person does is being kind and compassionate," Teddy continued. "A good person shares what they have with those who have less."

"I shared with Dora, who lives across the street. She didn't have a soccer ball, and I let her use mine," Jules said happily.

"A kind deed," Teddy said. "That is good. Show kindness and generosity every day."

"I will," Jules said. "I promise!"

"Perfect," Teddy smiled. "It's good to tell the truth, even when it is not popular or convenient or fun."

"I told a lie today," Jules said sadly. "That was why we were in time-out. I won't do that again."

"That's smart," Teddy said. "Learning from your mistakes is another thing that good people do. That way, they won't make those mistakes again. Now you know how important it is to tell the truth."

"I think I learned from my mistake today," Jules said. "I will try to always tell the truth from now on."

"That is very wise of you," Teddy smiled. "Let's see what else makes a person good. Oh, here's one, always think of how what you do will make other people feel."

"I know when I lied to Mommy, it made her sad," Jules said.

"So, when you are about to do or say something, think of the others around you. Think about how you will affect others."

"I will," Jules said. "I don't want to make other people sad or hurt their feelings."

"That's good," Teddy said. "After all, it's good to know that you are not the only person in the world, and everything you do can affect someone else. Another thing to remember is compassion and empathy. Even if you cannot help, it's good to have compassion for another person's situation."

"Like when I see a person with a broken arm," Jules said, "I feel sorry for them."

"That is excellent," Teddy said, feeling proud of his best friend. "That means that you have empathy and compassion. That is something that makes a good person."

"Really?" Jules said, "I didn't even try, I just felt sad for them!"

"Then you are just naturally empathetic and compassionate. You are ahead of the game! A good person also puts other's interests and needs ahead of their own," Teddy continued.

Jules thought about that for a moment. "I agreed to play with Chad in his treehouse, but I like mine better. Chad wasn't allowed to leave his house, so I went over to his. Does that count?"

"Yes, I think so," Teddy said thoughtfully. "You could have stayed here and played in your treehouse that you like better. Instead, you went over to Chad's house and played in his treehouse, which you didn't like as much. You did that to make a friend happy. Yes, I think that counts."

"Ok, good," Jules said. "I will make an effort to do that more."

"That is a good idea," Teddy said. "Keep doing that."

"I really want to be a good person, Teddy," Jules said. "I want Mommy and Daddy to be proud of me."

" But you already are a good person Jules," Teddy said. "Mommy and Daddy are already proud of you and they always will be. Just remember to stay a good person."

"So, to stay a good person," Jules said happily, "I just need to help others, be kind and compassionate, tell the truth, be considerate of others, be generous and giving. That doesn't sound too difficult."

"It's not too difficult," Teddy said. "It can get more difficult as we get older, but if you always think of those things, you will be just fine."

"I want to be a good person," Jules said, smiling.

"You are a good person," Teddy said. "I always thought so."

Jules and Teddy slept happily that night. Jules dreamed of saving kittens from trees, sharing with those less fortunate, standing up to bullies and doing other good deeds. Teddy knew that he was doing a great job being Jules' best friend. He was serving his purpose.

Sweet dreams little one.

Patience is a virtue. This statement is true. Everything worth doing takes patience. So many difficult tasks with great rewards require patience. And yet we are such an impatient species who constantly wish for immediate results. Everything we learn to do as we move through the various stages of life requires patience. But having patience can be difficult. We want what we want, and we want it now. But with patience, the reward, no matter if it is learning to walk, talk, read or even heal from an injury is so worth it. Patience must be taught, and that starts with those who teach us also being patient.

Oscar and Bridget were two very unique babies. They were twins, best friends, and on top of that, they were magical. Their parents were magicians, so it was only natural that Oscar and Bridget would have magic skills as well. From the moment the twins came home from the hospital, they showed magical abilities. If Oscar wanted a toy, all he needed to do was reach in its direction, and the toy would come to him floating through the air. If Bridget wanted Mommy, Mommy would appear. It was so easy. All the magic babies had to do was think of what they wanted, and it would magically happen.

Being that the babies were so gifted, it was not long before they started to talk. And once Oscar and Bridget began to speak, a whole new world opened up for them. Even though they could make things happen, they could now talk about making those things happen. Like all little kids, Oscar and Bridget loved to speak. They loved to talk to their parents. The twins loved to talk to each other. They spoke to other kids when they went out with their parents. The little twins talked so much that they even talked in their sleep. Sometimes when they would wake up, their bed would be covered with toys, or cats, or even soft cuddly bunnies. It was a great way to wake up. Of course, they would also have to put the toys away, but still, it was all fun.

Learning was fun and easy for Oscar and Bridget. Every discovery brought with it more knowledge and excitement. And of course, everything they learned gave Bridget and Oscar something new to talk about. The twins couldn't wait to learn more things. Especially walking and running. That looked like the best thing ever. Oscar wanted to run up and downhill. Bridget wanted to run into the sea and jump waves. The kids decided that walking and running must be the next thing that they would learn.

But learning to run and walk was different from learning to do other things. It was not something that they could simply decide to do. It required time and practice. Both Bridget and Oscar dreamed of running like the kids on the playground. It looked like such fun going down the sliding board, swinging on the swings, and building things in the sandbox. But to do all those things, the twins had to walk first. And that was the challenge.

Both twins were excellent at crawling and scooting around. The trouble came when they tried to stand up on their feet without help from their mother or father. It was easy to walk when they held hands and stood on Mommy or Daddy's feet. Even if they pulled up on a chair or table, the twins would still both fall on their bottoms. This happened each time they tried to stand up. Plop! They would fall right on their bottoms. After a while, it became very frustrating.

Oscar and Bridget watched their parents walk around the house. They watched kids running in the playground.

"Why can't we walk?" Oscar and Bridget both wondered.

"It looks like just about anyone can walk," Oscar said.

"So if anyone can do it, so can we," Bridget said.

"We just have to figure out how," Oscar said. "What is the best way to learn to walk?"

The twins decided to try using magic; after all, it worked on everything else. Focusing as he had never focused before, Oscar used his hands to pull himself up, he took a step. Bridget held her breath watching her brother. Flop! Oscar fell on his backside.

"Ow!" Oscar said as he hit the ground.

"Maybe I can do it," Bridget said, thinking that sometimes girls can do things that boys cannot. Then Bridget tried. She concentrated better than she ever had. Bridget used Daddy's big chair to pull herself up. Once she was up, she decided to take a step. Plop! Down she went on the ground.

"Ouch!" she said, feeling upset. "Perhaps we need to use some magic on each other."

"That might work," said Oscar. Bridget was always so smart, so when Oscar heard her suggestions, he always followed her advice.

"OK, so we will focus on each other instead of ourselves," Bridget said.

"Yes, didn't Mommy and Daddy say that we should never cast spells on ourselves?" Oscar said.

"That's right," Bridget said. "So, I will cast a spell on you, and you will cast a spell on me!"

Oscar and Bridget looked at each other, smiling. They agreed to focus on each other, perhaps their magic would work better if they did it that way.

First, Oscar focused on Bridget as she pulled herself up again. Once she was standing, Oscar said: "Now, walk, I command you!" Bridget took a step and Bonk! She fell on her bottom!

"Ouch!" Bridget said, rubbing her sore bottom.

"We might need to pad ourselves with pillows or something," Oscar said. "If this doesn't work, we should think about doing that. Otherwise, we might never be able to sit down again!"

"Let me try," Bridget said. Perhaps her magic was stronger than Oscar's.

Bridget concentrated all her magic at Oscar. Using the sofa, Oscar pulled himself up carefully and slowly. When he was finally standing, Bridget said: "Now, Oscar, walk, I command you!" Oscar smiled and took a step. And Wup! He fell right down on his bottom again.

"If we don't walk soon, we are going to have to put pillows in our pants!" Bridget said. "Just like you said!"

"Or have Mommy and Daddy put pillows

everywhere so that we don't bruise!" Oscar said. He imagined what their home would look like covered with pillows. Oscar sort of liked the idea because it sounded fun. But he also really wanted to walk. He wanted to run even more.

"Why is this so difficult?" asked Bridget to her brother. She had never found anything so complicated.

"I don't know," Oscar said. "Everything else is easy. We are magicians. We can make anything happen."

"But not walking," Bridget said. "Why can't we walk?"

"Maybe we aren't using the correct magic," said Oscar thoughtfully. "Let's try something different."

They tried a few more times with no luck. The twins tried focusing harder. They tried to concentrate in different ways. Instead of saying, "Walk, I command you," they said, "Now, please walk." Bridget tried using her sparkly wand. Oscar tried using magic fairy dust. Finally, both Bridget and Oscar were too exhausted to keep trying and they were both so frustrated that they started to cry. This is what babies do when they get upset, even magic babies.

Mommy and Daddy ran over and hugged Bridget and Oscar.

“What is the matter, sweet babies?” Mommy asked.

“Are you hurt?” asked Daddy.

“No! I can’t walk!” cried Bridget.

“No! I can’t run!” cried Oscar.

“It’s alright,” Mommy said. “It can be hard to learn to walk.”

“I want to run!” Oscar cried.

“Me too!” cried Bridget. Running did sound better than walking.

“I understand,” Daddy said. “But you have to learn to walk before you can run.”

“And we don’t learn to walk until we are ready,” Mommy said, “It just takes time. You just have to practice and be patient.”

“And,” Daddy said, “We will help you.”

“That’s it! We need your magic!” Bridget cheered.

"Yes, go ahead! Cast your spells on us!" Oscar said. "Command us to walk! We are ready!" And both twins prepared for their parents' magic to make them walk.

"Walking has nothing to do with magic," Daddy said. "That is something that takes lots of practice."

"But we will help you practice," Mommy laughed.

Each day, Mommy and Daddy helped the twins to try to walk. They practiced with Bridget and Oscar walking on their feet while holding hands. They also helped each twin practice standing up. Every day, Oscar and Bridget practiced and practiced and practiced again. Each time, Plop! They fell on their bottoms. But, with the encouragement of their parents, the twins kept trying.

After two weeks, the twins were both tired and frustrated. They still had not been able to take a step. Both Oscar and Bridget felt like giving up. But Mommy said, "You have to be patient, remember, things like walking and running take time." Then, she hugged both Oscar and Bridget. "I love you both so much."

"Maybe they need a break," Daddy suggested.

"No! We are going to do this!" both twins said at the same time.

"Well, alright," Mommy said. "Let's keep trying."

"We will try five more times," Daddy said. "Then, we have some ice-cream."

"But what if we can't do it?" asked Bridget. The ice cream was a great reward, but at the rate they were going, Bridget imagined there would be no reward of any kind.

"That doesn't matter," Mommy said. "We can get ice cream no matter what."

And so, the twins tried five more times. Each time, Plop! Down they went. Bridget and Oscar were tired and feeling defeated. The ice cream tasted delicious and made the twins feel a little better.

The next day, Mommy and Daddy took Bridget and Oscar to the park. They put them on the swings where they encouraged the twins to pump with their legs. Then Mommy and Daddy both helped the kids to go down the slide, making sure that both twins used their legs to slow down. After the park, the family went out for more ice cream.

"I think that you guys need a break," Mommy said as she ate her ice cream, which was strawberry.

"If we take a break, we may never learn!" Oscar

said as he ate his mint chocolate chip cone.

“How can stopping and taking a break help?” asked Bridget, licking her chocolate peanut butter cone.

“Sometimes, we need to step away from something to figure it out,” Daddy explained cheerfully, enjoying his mango sorbet. “That way, when you go back to work, you are fresh as you approach the problem.”

Bridget and Oscar continued to eat their ice-cream and thought about what Daddy said.

“That makes sense,” Bridget said.

“Yes,” Oscar agreed. “We will have more energy after taking a break.”

And so, the twins continued to enjoy their ice-cream and tried to not think about how they could not yet walk. Or run.

That night, at home, everyone sat down to watch telly. Oscar was seated at the end of the sofa. Bridget was sitting on the ground with the cat.

“Oscar, could you bring me the remote?” Daddy asked.

Without thinking, Oscar got down and wobbled over holding the remote.

“Oscar! You’re walking!” Bridget cheered! Then, Bonk! Oscar fell on his bottom when he realized that he was walking.

Bridget stood up, using the table for help. She tottered over to where Oscar had fallen, and she plopped down too. The two started laughing, and then both stood up using Daddy’s chair and teetered back to where they had been sitting.

“Now, we both can walk!” Bridget laughed.

“And we did it together!” Oscar cheered.

“Yes, you did!” said Mommy. “We knew you could do it! It just took time and patience!”

“Now we have to learn to run!” said Oscar before falling again.

That night, Oscar and Bridget fell asleep with smiles on their faces. Both dreamt of running through clouds, racing with cheetahs and dancing with bumblebees. Bridget dreamed of running and dancing with fairies. Oscar imagined that he was running on water.

Sweet dreams little one.

Chapter 3 Fantastic Characters

A MERMAID'S MEMORY

Cora was a lovely mermaid who lived along a coastal paradise in Whimsy. She was a curious and brave mermaid who lived her life adventurously. She was a sight behold and left many unsuspecting sailors gasping in their tracks. Cora had dark skin and eyes, which contrasted her silky pink hair. Her high cheekbones lent to her elegance and made her the very embodiment of feminine beauty.

Cora was hundreds of years old but still looked to be in the throes of her youth. Strangers would always refer to her age when speaking to her; this amused her, so she never corrected them. She had been around for so long that she was well known throughout the kingdom. She was also one of the most amiable of her species, which meant that whenever anyone had a message for the mermaids, they would find Cora.

The curious mermaid was fascinated by the world around her. She lived in a deep part of the ocean with her family. The mermaid people had formed a community that stayed in the caverns that littered an underwater mountain. She loved all the rich colors that the ocean hosted. She even found beauty in the depths of blackness when she traveled so far underwater that not even sunlight could penetrate the eternal night. Every fish at that level was made of some sort of bioluminescent material; it was a natural light show.

Cora would also follow boats around from a safe distance, watching as the sailors laughed and joked with one another. She found mortals to be endlessly entertaining, but knew how dangerous they could be. One particularly frightening incident occurred when she was following one of these vessels, and she was spotted. The men on board decided that they would try to catch her. They would no doubt have put her on display somewhere or treated her like a pet of some sort.

This was a fear that always lurked in the back of a mermaid's mind. History had not always been very kind to those with fishtails. She was as cautious as she could, but she just could not give up her exploring.

One day Cora was patrolling the waters near the shore with the other mermaids. They would gather trash from the seafloor and assist any animal who was tangled up in something that a boat or tourist had discarded. This was part of their duty as humanoid fish, to clear the seas and try to make the ocean better for all who lived there.

She noticed a rather large fish that seemed to be lying completely skill on the seafloor. It seemed to be tangled up in a fisherman's net that had been thrown out. She felt a sting of sadness for the poor fish. Cora then noticed a flicking in its tail; it was still very much alive.

She rushed over to the injured fish and began trying to free it from this net. The animal did not understand that she was trying to help it and began to flail around violently. It thrashed from side to side, causing a storm of bubbles and chaos.

Cora was slowly realizing that she was in a dangerous situation. She began to panic as she tried to escape some of the fish's blows. Once she had gotten a safe distance from it, she decided to go and find a knife to cut the net and free the wild and terrifying creature.

She knew that finding such an item without venturing back to her cave was a long shot, but luckily for her, there was the next best thing. She scanned the ocean floor for a tooth. The sharks in Whimsy are gigantic, which has never come in handy for anyone until right this moment. She found one as large as her hand and jagged enough to get the job done.

She approached the worried fish again, this time looking a bit like she was going to stab it. The poor thing was so panicked that it began its exhaustive thrashing again, jerking back and forth. Cora probably should have hidden the frightening tooth until she was behind the fish's field of vision.

The mermaid managed to cut a few pieces of the net, and the fish seemed to be trying to wiggle free. That is when disaster struck for Cora, though, as the terrifying creature was still creating a visible storm of bubbles. She felt a strong fin smash her against a rock. She was swallowed by the struggle for a moment.

She felt herself taking on the tangle that the fish was shuffling off. Its constant fighting and flipping were causing her to become more and more entrapped in the net. Cora was unable to move very much at all. The fish slammed into her again, forcing her head into the same rock. Cora watched as the ocean around her dimmed and turned black.

When she awoke, she was drifting helplessly along an underwater stream. She quickly figured out her location, and panic ensued. She was soon going to be swept up in the crashing waves and roughed up some more, before being deposited on the shore. This should not happen. There were too many things that could go wrong, and mermaids tend to avoid the beach whenever they can because it makes them sitting ducks. Some days are safer than others, but she was going to have no idea ahead of time.

Cora was unable to maneuver the crashing waves and was thrown about yet again. She was completely restrained and at the mercy of fate. There was nothing that the poor mermaid could do, except to brace herself for the inevitable impact. She was dragged along the broken shells in the shallow water and finally laid down rather gently on the beautiful sand.

It seemed like an eternity passed as she was lying exposed on the beach, with no one in sight. She was beginning to give up any hope of being taken back to the sea by high tide. She noticed a small young figure in the distance. A boy was approaching, and she could make out the exact moment that he noticed her.

He stopped in his tracks and then began running toward Cora. She was both frightened and overjoyed because no matter what was going to happen, at least this horrible experience would soon be over. He crouched over the mermaid, looking very concerned. He told her that his name was Eddie and then asked her what he could do to help.

Cora was almost too weak to speak and was unable to do anything but mumble. Adult voices rang out just behind them, which seemed to worry Eddie even more. He told the mermaid that his father was just over the hill behind them. His father was a curator for a museum.

The mermaid was fading in and out of consciousness but knew that the boy's statement meant that she was still in mortal danger. As a child, she had so many nightmares about being captured and placed on display for the public to gawk at. This was shaping up to be one of the worst days of her life.

The young boy then pulled out a pocket knife and began sawing at various parts of the net, breaking the links as quickly as he could. He was frantic about the actions, so she understood that her fears about his father were justified. Eddie jerked the mermaid around to free her from the remaining tangles just as his father and another man appeared over the hill. The man screamed for Eddie to stop right away and back up.

The young man paused briefly and then

continued to strip the net from Cora. He told her that he was sorry for what he was about to do. Eddie was too small to pick up a grown woman, so he did the best thing that he could do in that situation and began rolling her back toward the tide. His father was running down the hill toward the two of them. The moment that the water touched Cora's skin; she found her motivation again.

The mermaid clawed and fought her way through the broken shells and crashing waves. She darted below the surface of the water and swam back to safety as quickly as she could. Once she was a reasonable distance away from the beach, she turned around to see the father strike Eddie out of anger. She wished more than anything that she could thank the young man for saving her life. She had no idea at the time, but she would get her chance.

On a hot July day, some twenty years later, Cora was following a vessel of sailors that was exploring a nearby island. She was concerned for this operation because the island was known for its jagged and unforgiving shore. She kept a safe distance behind the boat, hoping for its sake that it would just turn around.

The boat did no such thing though and was dashed against one of the nastiest looking rocks. It splintered in half and was repeatedly slammed into the same stony protrusions. Cora never gave up on helping others, no matter how dangerous the situation was. She swam to the sailor's aid at once. She found him beaten up and floating toward the bottom of the ocean.

The mermaid hoisted him up above her, which was easier said than done. She swam the only path of safety to the island. This was a trail through the jagged rocks that no one knew about, except the creatures that inhabited the waters near the island. Cora laid the sailor down and began to perform chest compressions to bring him back. She was seated right at the water's edge so that she would not dry out while attempting to save his life.

The sailor coughed and then spat out a good deal of water. He was worse for wear from the incident, but he was alive. As he regained consciousness, he blinked heavily. Then his eyes widened at the sight of the mermaid, which is a normal reaction. Except in this case.

"You!" The man said, still coughing in-between gasps.

"Me?" Cora said, putting the back of her hand against the stranger's forehead.

"It's me, Eddie..." He said, looking utterly lost. Cora's mouth fell open at this statement. The boy who had saved her all those years ago.

Cora was happy to meet Eddie again, because in all those years of regret that she couldn't say thank you for what he did.

The sense of gratitude that was felt had driven her throughout her life to generous both with and help everyone she could. Cora knew that someone's help can help save your life!

This was her chance to finally thank him for his actions. As the two laid there on the beach amazed at their luck, fate smiled down upon them.

Gratitude is something that fills your heart with joy!

A FAIRY PRINCESS

The nights in Whimsy have been strange lately. There was an eeriness in the air that seemed to permeate through the darkness. Every night around the stroke of midnight, a melancholy voice rang out through the hills. No one spoke of it at first; every creature assumed that they would be called crazy.

It happened night after night, and eventually there was no way that anyone could deny hearing the song. It was haunting and slow, vibrating around the emptiness. Ghostly and forlorn, it captured the imagination of every child in the land.

Many thought that it might be a spirit, mourning its life from beyond the grave. There was also a banshee theory going around the dragon Timmy community. The elves thought that it must be a magical creature calling out for help, someone who was too afraid to ask during the day.

One thing was certain, though; it was the most beautiful voice to ever sweep over Whimsy. The fullness of this disembodied female voice was unmistakable. Those who woke up to listen to it were moved to tears. The relatable despondency in the tone drove some of the more creative creatures to paint what they thought the singer might look like. Others wrote plays about the voice, trying to provide a backstory for the unusual sound.

Search parties were formed to try and locate the source once she had started her nightly singing. No matter where they roamed, they were unable to find her. The sound was bouncing off too many mountains. The elves communed with Mother Nature to ask for her guidance. Whoever the singer was, Nature was keeping her secret.

Rom the dragon, Timmy and his friend Blue (an elf) decided to fly over the land and see if they could find the voice. They tried this to no avail; it was difficult to get a good view of the ground in the darkness. Rumors raged on for months, and no one had any clue where the sound was coming from.

Whoever was singing hardly got any sleep at all; this became the running joke in Whimsy. Whenever someone would yawn, they would be jokingly accused of being the night singer. Other jokes asserted that her voice was so beautiful that she must look like a toad. Otherwise, there is no balance in the universe.

There was an official inquiry launched by the fairies. They wanted to make sure that the sad singer was mentally sound. The fairies organized all the creatures in groups and assigned each an area to search. This was the first official effort to locate the voice. Every creature was given light so that they could still see in the dark.

It was Rom and Blue who first located the source of the voice. It belonged to the famous fairy princess May, standing on top of a mountain and singing into the ether. She was surprised to see the pair landing beside her. May was mostly disconnected from the rest of Whimsy, so she had no idea that her voice was being heard all over the realm. It shouldn't have been able to carry that far. It's almost as though the wind was sympathetic to her plight.

The fairy princess was not tiny like her subjects. She was a fully-grown woman, which was one of the privileges associated with wearing the crown. May was angelic looking and had long captivated Whimsy. Creatures would flock from all over to hear her speeches. She lived in a dreamy castle on a hilltop with her father and mother, the king and queen.

They passed along their rather peculiarly regal looks to the young lady. She had a head of stark white hair that shone like a halo around her pale face. She was ghostly but elegant and beautiful. Wearing a white nightgown, she looked rather like a displaced spirit telling her woes to the wind.

Upon seeing the sad face of the princess, the

two friends embraced her. She began to sob with relief that someone had finally heard her calls. May thought that she would suffer alone forever. She also felt weak for being so upset during such a great time of peace in her land.

Rom allowed her and Blue to climb on his back. They would take her to the elven forest and call the fairies for a meeting. She was embarrassed that such a fuss was going to be made on her behalf, but she also wanted help. May was so tired, she needed rest, and yet it would not come.

When everyone had arrived at the elven village, they began to discuss the nature of her sadness. The elves and the fairies formed a council that would work together to ensure that the princess was taken care of and happy again. May told them that she could not sleep and hadn't been able to for some time. She said that she worried about her people and the rest of the land very much.

She was made anxious by all the bad things that happen in the world, and singing was the only way for her to get any of that fear out. She wanted to find a healthier way to deal with her stress, but nothing she had tried so far has worked. She was nervous all the time.

This was the elves' area of expertise, and they were enthusiastically willing to help the princess.

She looked helpless, sitting among that giant group of magical creatures; she felt that they were all dissecting her thoughts. She must look like such a child to them, she thought.

Quite the contrary, being anxious is normal. The elves were nervous by nature, as many creatures of intelligence are. They had mastered a method to deal with those feelings too, something that helped no matter how bad things got. They assigned the young princess a trainer who would begin working with her tomorrow morning. Until then, she was given sleeping tea and flown back to her tower.

Her trainer was an elf that others called Indigo. He told May that he was going to show her something that worked for him when he was having a hard time. He told her to sit down with her legs crossed. She was to become aware of her feet, and then relax them. Then he told her to become aware of her calf muscles and then relax them. He kept going all the way up the princess's body. Every muscle group addressed, she should draw her attention to it and then relax it.

Next, she was told to inhale slowly, as much air as she possibly could. She should concentrate only on the air that she is breathing in. When her lungs are full of air, she would then begin slowly breathing out of her nose.

The elf told her to do this every single morning and every night before she wanted to sleep. He said that as she got better at it, he would show her some more advanced techniques. He taught the young princess how to meditate.

She followed his advice upon her return home, and it helped so much. He was also going to function as a counselor for her, which also seemed to be making a difference. May had felt like she could not talk to anyone about her problems and now she finally had someone to talk to.

To thank the fairies and elves for their help, she arranged a concert for all the creatures of Whimsy who had fallen in love with her voice. She sang the songs of summer, love and friendship. Her voice united every soul in Whimsy and would go down in history.

THE PRINCESS AND THE THIEF

Now it's time for you to get ready to crawl into bed and get all snuggly and warm; are you ready? Okay, make sure your pillow is good and fluffed. You want the fluff of the pillow to keep all the good dreams in and to keep all the bad dreams out. Now, lay your head into the pillow and shimmy, shimmy, shimmy, until you're nice and snuggled in. Pull your blankets up to your chin and snuggle in all snug. Do you have a fluffy friend you like to keep in bed with you? Let's get that fluffy friend into the covers with you. There, now you're nice and ready!

Close your little eyes and breathe big and deep. Breathe in through your nose nice and slow, then hold your breath for just a second. Now let it out slowly and feel it taking all those wiggles away with it. You're all wiggled out, you're ready for a nice sleep, and you're feeling calm.

Now, it's time to say goodbye to the thoughts that are in your mind. Tell those thoughts, "Thank you for visiting, but it's time for you to go now. I will see you in the morning when we're all shiny and fresh." Let those thoughts go away for the night so you can focus on the story we're about to tell. When I count to three, those thoughts are going to whoosh, fly away. Right out the window, they will go, and they will come back in the morning when you're ready for them. 1... 2... 3... There. Now we're ready for a nice story that will take us on an adventure and get us ready for some happy dreams.

Imagine that you are floating in a river made out of fluffy blankets. They're soft and warm and flowing down. Just down the river, you can see that the fluffy blankets drop into a short little waterfall. Whee! You slide down the blankets and start to fly into the air, flying up into the night sky. There are stars all around you, twinkling and blinking brightly like shiny diamonds.

In front of you, you can see a blue light. At first, it looks like a small light, but as you get closer, you realize that it looks very big. It's wavy and shiny, almost like a pool in the summertime sun. You touch the wavy blue light, and you feel yourself being pulled into it gently. You slide through the light and into a big castle. This is where you hear the story about the princess and the thief.

The princess lived in the castle that sat just at the center of a bustling town. She looked out her window as she worked on her sewing. She looked at the people in the town running around, doing their shopping, walking their animals and living their lives. She had wanted to go out and do things with the people in the town, but her parents were always telling her about the things that she needed to do in the castle instead.

Any time she wanted to go out into the town and try something new, there was something new that her parents insisted she had to do before she could go. Every time this happened, the task she started kept her in the castle until well after sundown, when there were no more fun things to do in the town with the townspeople. She decided that she would stop asking, as it seemed like her parents would never let her go out into the world to try new things.

As she looked down at the town, she thought she noticed something weird about the way the townspeople were acting. It seemed like something was going on that had disturbed the townspeople. People were running around, the sheriff and his men were out and talking to people in the town, and things didn't look like they normally did.

Normally, things looked very calm in the town square. People walked to and from places without too much hurry, and they always seemed to be time for the people in the square to talk with one another. Now, it seemed like people were rushing around.

"What's going on down there, Agatha?" The maid in the princess's chamber looked out the window and then back at the sewing she was doing.

"There's a thief in the town who has been stealing things from people. No one knows who he is, but there are a lot of things missing. It's for the best that you're safe in here with all these guards, so he doesn't steal anything important from you or the king and queen, isn't it?"

The princess could tell that Agatha was just trying to get her to feel better about not getting to leave the castle, but she just wanted to know more about the thief. She wanted to know who he was, what he was taking, why he was taking it, and she wanted to know what it was like for him to steal from other people. Sure, it was wrong, and no one should ever do it, but there must be a reason he was doing it, right? Maybe he needed some help. Maybe the princess could help him with the troubles that made him start stealing in the first place.

The princess was always looking for ways to help the people in the town, and she was always looking for more ways to connect with people. Staying in the castle away from everyone could be very lonely and she knew that if she could talk to the people in the town, she could make a big difference and she could help them to live better lives.

Agatha stood up and walked out of the room to get lunch for the princess. The princess sat watching out the window when she heard a noise. She turned in her chair to see a young man standing behind her curtains on the other side of the room.

"Who are you?" The princess was afraid, but she didn't want to show it to this strange person in her room.

"I'm Claudius. I'm sorry to be in your room like this, but I needed to get away from the sheriff and his guards. I'm the thief that they've been talking about, but it's not what you think. Please, I need your help." The princess looked at him for a moment and then stood up to show him to a secret door in her room.

"Follow these steps to my library, and I will come to meet you tonight when my maids have gone and when people have calmed down. Can you wait that long?" The young man nodded and followed the stairs to the library, just as the Princess said.

The princess carried on through her day, trying not to let anyone know that there was something or someone she was hiding from them. As the sun started to set, she got excited about meeting with the man in her library to help him. She had only been able to help a couple of people in her life, and she enjoyed how it made her feel. Because of that, she couldn't wait to talk to someone else who needed her help.

When the time came, she went to the library to find the thief asleep in one of the chairs. She gently nudged his foot, and he leaped out of the chair with great surprise.

“I’m sorry! I didn’t mean to scare you. Please explain what’s going on and how I can help!” The thief calmed down for a moment and caught his breath.

“A witch sent me here. My mother sent me to the witch to get a magical spell or potion that would help my family get through the winter. The witch sent me here to get something for her, but everyone who has seen me has accused me of stealing things that I never touched. People I’ve never seen before are calling me a thief and saying I stole all their valuable things!”

“Oh my, that’s terrible. What did the witch send you here to get? Maybe I can help you to find it.”

“She was not very clear about what it is, but she said that it would come to me when I needed it. I feel as though I need it now. She said I would need ‘a kiss of amber.’ I have no idea what it means, but I’ve been looking for just about anything amber-colored that I can find.” The princess stared at him for a moment. “What?”

“My name is Amber.”

"Oh, I see. So, if you kiss me, then my poor family will have enough food and shelter to last us through the winter?"

"I don't know how the witch's magic works. It sounds like that might be right. If you weren't meant to find me, I don't know why you would have ended up in my castle. Maybe everyone thinking you stole from them was her way of driving you into the castle for safety, bringing you closer to me."

"You might be onto something with that idea. Still, I mean no disrespect at all about all of this, and if you don't want to kiss me, I understand. I will go home and find another way to help my family. Please don't worry."

"No, I want to help. After all, if I can help with something as simple as a kiss... I think I should do that. It's my job to look after the people who live in this kingdom, and if a kiss is how I will do that, then so be it!" The princess stood in the middle of the library with her eyes closed tight and her lips puckered. After a couple of seconds in the silence, the princess opened her eyes to see Claudius standing on the other side of the library, looking guilty.

"Is everything okay?"

"I feel guilty, your highness. I want to give you

something in return, but I have nothing. You don't even know me, yet you're willing to do this for me. I am touched, but I am also ashamed."

"Please don't worry," The princess said "I can never leave the castle to help the people in my kingdom. This is my chance to make a difference in the life of at least one person."

"Oh, it would. It would make a difference in the lives of my entire family - my mother, father, brother and sister."

"I'm so happy to hear that. So please. This is something that I want to do for you and your family."

Claudius smiled and nodded. The princess once again closed her eyes and puckered her lips. Claudius touched his lips to hers for just a moment, and a glittering, swirling magic filled the room. It was like a million little fairies swirled into the room, sweeping all the air into a frenzy. The air smelled like berries and sweet fruit and both Amber and Claudius felt their hearts beginning to swell.

When the magic settled and the room went back to its dim lighting, Claudius and Amber looked at each other. It was like they could see gold speckles in each other's eyes that made them feel like home. They were instantly in love.

“What... What is this feeling?” Claudius couldn’t pull his stare away from Amber’s eyes.

“I think this is true love,” she answered.

Just then, a candle in the middle of the room flickered to life. The flame grew and grew and grew until it turned green and the witch’s face appeared in it.

“You have found the kiss of Amber that I sent you to find. You two have been destined for one another, the fates have decided! I helped you to reach her early so that you may find each other before this very hard winter. Now your true love can help your family, and you may all survive the bitter cold. As for my payment... Please tell the king’s most trusted wizard that ‘Hildy says hello,’ he’ll know what it means.”

And just like that, poof. The candle went out and all that was left in the room was Amber and Claudius and their true love.

Everyone forgot about their “stolen things,” and Claudius was free of any pointing fingers. Soon, the two went to the king and confessed their love for one another to get his blessing. Soon they were married, and Claudius brought his mother, father, brother and sister to live in a nice, warm castle.

They all lived happily ever after.

The End

THE PRINCESS UNDER THE SEA

There once was a lovely young woman who lived in the sea. She was born in the sea and knew only of its properties and its abundance. Her father was the King of the Realm and guarded her aggressively, as he loved her more than life itself.

Her name was Ari, and she was a mermaid. Ari often swam close to the land and then popped up to the surface to watch the men on the beach and in the neighboring town. She was lonely and had begun to feel restless with her life under the sea. She wanted so very badly to walk like the land women she saw on the beach and to find a land man who would love her and want to take care of her forever.

One day, she went to see her Father's Sorcerer and told him about her dreams and her desires. The Sorcerer was aware that the King had forbidden her to even speak of the land species, and that he was never going to allow her to leave the safety of the water. He knew that, and she knew that, but he came up with a plan, and on the following week, he called Ari to his chamber.

Ari was intrigued by the Sorcerers plan and became very excited. She had been spending more time than ever watching the people on the beach, and she knew that she would never be happy until she was able to go forth unto the world of the walking and find her mate. She listened carefully, as the wicked Sorcerer outlined his plan and agreed to all its terms. The plan was kept a secret from the King, as she knew her Father would lock her in her chamber for an eternity if he found out. She had the Sorcerer make a potion that she would drink and become a land lady - but there was a catch. She would only be able to stay a land lady for one week before she would again turn into a mermaid.

On the day she had set aside to swim to the water's edge and then drink the potion, she made herself look as pretty as she possibly could, and then left the King's domain. As she swam nearer to the water's edge, she became nervous. "What if the potion does not work, and I get stuck on land forever? What if the potion does work and I become old and ugly and stuck on land forever?" she thought. Then she said to herself, "You are just being silly. The King's Sorcerer is the finest Sorcerer; he would never make such a ridiculous mistake."

Ari swam on her back for some time going over what it would be like to be human, to walk on two legs and do human things like fall in love. "Fall in love," she whispered to herself; "Fall in love?" Yes, that is what she wanted, so she would go ahead and drink the potion. With that, she pulled out the vial the Sorcerer had given her and drank the entire thing. Then, she began to feel very strange, but in a very good way. Her vision blurred for a moment, and she felt light-headed and drifty. Then everything changed, and she felt as though she had been sleeping all her life and now woke up. She felt elated, alive and excited at the same time.

Ari looked around at the beach again; only this time, the beach looked like where she would have to go if she wanted to go home, and the deep ocean looked like a place to go if she wanted to explore. "The potion has worked beyond all my expectations!" she thought to herself. "And now, for the ultimate test of its power," she thought as she looked down at her tail. The tail was nowhere to be seen and in its place were two long, slender, and beautiful legs. "This will do nicely!" she exclaimed aloud, "Very nicely."

She immediately began swimming for the shore, and for the very first time in all of her years, she put her feet down and felt the sandy bottom, the sand between her toes and the movement of legs and feet. Something she had been dreaming about for so very long. Ari was now in the shallow waters near the very edge of the ocean, where it meets the sandy beach. She looked at the beach now only a matter of feet from her and watched as the water lapped up and down on the seashore. It was a beautiful sight to her as she could never have come this close to land before when she had a tail instead of these two wonderful legs, as she could have easily become stranded and then discovered by the humans. Everyone had warned all the children in the realm that if the humans ever caught them, they would poke and prod them and put them in cages and treat them like freaks. "Nobody should ever have to endure such treatment," the king had taught them.

But now, she could easily just walk out of the water and onto the beach and talk to whomever she pleased. Her time had come and so, for the very first time in her life, she placed her two new feet on the sandy bottom, leaned forward to put all of her body weight over them, and pushed up. For the very first time in her life, she was standing, and she loved this new feeling. "This is great!" she called out aloud. "What is great?" a man's voice asked nearby. Ari was shocked and stunned. She had never heard a real man's voice spoken over the air of the planet. She turned to see an old man wearing a pair of ugly bathing trunks standing not 20 feet from her. "Oh, hello," she said. "I was just planning a party for my husband," she lied, "And I thought of a great way to surprise him." She continued. "Oh, so it's a surprise party, eh?" the man muttered. "What? Oh Uh... yes, that's right. A surprise party for my husband."

And then she turned and walked for the very first time. She walked like a real woman that she indeed was on that day. She walked with confidence. She walked with character and charisma.

"But where was she walking to?" she began to wonder. "Oh no," she thought. "I did not think this through very well. Now, what do I do?" she asked herself.

She saw a small building with a palm leaf roof and noticed that there were a lot of people sitting on highchairs and leaning on a long platform. They were all facing the same way and laughing and talking, and most of them were men. "Right." She said to herself. "I'll go there and join them."

As she approached the shack, most of the men suddenly became all in a bother and began shuffling around to look at her. One of them let out a strange whistling sound that came from his mouth. "Well, hello there, sweetheart!" the closest one said. "Hey there, honey. There's an open seat here by me. And it's open forever for you, baby!" another one claimed. She noticed all the men were asking for her company except for one. As it happened, he was way down at the other end of the platform and was very handsome. She headed towards him and was in luck. There was an open seat on the very end of the platform on the other side of the man. She walked right up to it across the sandy beach and climbed up into that highchair.

There was another man whom she had not noticed on the other side of the platform, and he had on a funny outfit. It was not a bathing suit like all the men on her side had on, but had bright red and white colors on it and was quite ugly. She tensed when she saw the strange man behind the platform walking straight towards her. “What’ll it be, miss?” the man asked her. She froze. She had no idea what he was asking her or why he was even talking to her.

She just stared at him for a moment and then said, “I don’t know,” which was the truth. He thought she meant she didn’t know what she wanted and said, “Okay miss, I’ll check back with you in a few minutes,” and went back to fiddling with his glasses and bottles. The gentleman whom she had sat beside turned to look at her, and she found herself hypnotized by his bright blue eyes, his dark curly hair and his smile.

Then he spoke. “I’m John Blake,” he said, and then he waited. She knew she was supposed to say something, but she didn’t know what. Her name! That was it; he wanted to meet her. Of course! “I’m Ari,” she said finally and then turned to face forward again. He did not stop looking at her, and in fact, he held out his hand in a way she had never seen. His thumb was facing up, his little finger down and his hand was stiff like a knife. She turned and made her hand into the same gesture. He looked down at both of them, holding their hands out in a ridiculous fashion and quickly took her hand with his and bobbed their hands up and down a few times and then let go of it. "How strange," she thought.

A little more time passed, and then the handsome Mr. Blake turned towards her again and said, "I was wondering if you would like to join me for a walk on the beach?" Ari's face lit up because this was something she did understand, and she liked this man very much. "I would love to," she answered with a smile. The two slid off their barstools and walked down towards the water and then down the beach. They walked and talked for over an hour and became good friends. Then, she noticed that he was a little bit nervous, and she guessed that she was too. This was wonderful. She had walked out of the water and into the life of a tall, handsome stranger.

Then suddenly, out of the blue, John asked her, "May I buy you dinner tonight?" Before she knew what she was doing, she agreed, but there was a problem. The Sorcerer had forgotten to provide her with the whole story. She needed clothes and money and who knew what else to function on dry land. Realizing that she was in a bit of a jam, she quickly made up a story about how she had been on vacation with some girlfriends and had become separated from them.

That day, they were scheduled to board a bus somewhere and get to the airport, and now all she had were the clothes on her back and nowhere to stay. He bought the story and took care of everything. They went to the clothing store and purchased some fine items for her and then went to dinner. After dinner, she went home with him, and he let her stay on his couch, but before long, they fell in love, and he wanted her to stay forever. Of course, she couldn't do that, but continued to make up stories about why.

Eventually, they became very happy together, and he began asking questions she had no answers for. This made her very uncomfortable, so she decided to tell him the truth. "You're a Mermaid?" he said with an astonished look on his face. Ari was amazed at how well he took this incredible information and was then even more in love with him. How would they do it? What could they do to make it work now that he knew her complete truth? Then John had an idea. He told her that he was a scuba diver, and he asked her what she thought of him coming into the water for some visits, and then she could come on land on other visits.

That plan seemed like the only one that could work. "I'll buy a sailboat," he said. "And I can pick you up, and you can be yourself and be with me on the boat. We can sail around and have lunch, and well, what do you think?" he asked. She was overjoyed at the thought of having honesty between them and agreed.

In the months that followed, John and Ari spent every spare moment together. Sometimes swimming together and playing in the ocean and sometimes sailing which, as it happened, she loved. She had never been on a real sailboat, and John was a great sailor. Then one day, she went to the Sorcerer and asked him if he could change her permanently into a land walker. He was very worried about what the king would think, but then figured out a way to make it so she had control over her body. She could be herself in the water and share precious moments with her father, and she could be the land girl and be with her man whenever she liked.

Soon, John asked her to marry him, and after learning what marriage meant, she was very happy to marry him. As time went on, Ari spent most of her time with John, and just enough time with her father, so he did not suspect anything or get angry because she was spending so much time away.

But Ari became more and more sad because she didn't like have a double life: she felt as a liar!

So one day she decided to confront her father and tell him the whole truth.

The father at first became very angry but then, seeing his lovely daughter so sincere and determined to become forever a human to follow her love, he surrendered and with his eyes to tears gave his permission.

In the end, she had three wonderful children, and to her relief, they all had human legs and were perfect babies. She was sad that she could not live with her Father in the great sea, but happy that she had achieved her dreams beyond what she had ever thought possible.

Ari had a wonderful family with a loving husband and three adorable children!

That was how our story went, and anyone who read it was charmed by the little girl who grew up as a Mermaid and one day did meet her prince charming.

Never let go of your dreams!

THE HAPPIEST MERMAID

In this sleep meditation story, imagine meeting the happiest mermaid in the secret rainbow reef of the beautiful deep blue ocean. If you are curious to find out why this friendly and lovely creature is known as the happiest mermaid, then settle in and relax because you're in for a fun and inspiring journey of ocean dreams and mermaid magic. Imagine a tiny tropical island in the beautiful ocean, three palm trees, pure white sands with some lovely ocean shells and a washed-up starfish. Your tropical island is in a secret spot in the Great Barrier Reef off the coast of Australia in the middle of a turquoise blue lagoon.

Breathe slowly and deeply... Can you imagine a wonderful white beach? Hot sand and small waves that wet your feet? What a wonderful feeling!

Here the waters are shallow and calm. You

feel so excited to be here because these warm and healing waters are home to some of the most wonderful coral gardens in the world. Also, it is home to one of the loveliest and rarest of ocean creatures. Imagine walking across the warm white sands and feeling the sand squish in between your toes, which is so relaxing and connects you to the energy of nature. Now imagine picking up a soft velvety starfish, which happens to be your favorite color, as it smiles up at you with its cute little face. You step into the ocean water which is so pure and clear and healthy.

It cleanses your mind and quenches your soul.

You gently toss the little starfish out into the calm ocean waves, and it makes a happy little splash to be back in the sea. Now you see a second splash as something beautiful emerges out of the ocean waves. Your heart flutters with surprise and joy as you see a real live mermaid before your eyes. She is bobbing up and down in the waves and smiling curiously at you. Feeling very lucky to be meeting a mystical mermaid, you admire her long, shiny hair and her open, friendly face. You notice that she is about the same age as you and seems like such a lovely mermaid girl.

You can tell from the way she is splashing about happily that she loves to have lots of fun. You wave to her, and she instantly waves back happily. Now you see sparkles of enchantment twinkling and shimmering around you as this magical energy of pure love and nature dances around you. Suddenly, you realize you are no longer standing in the water, but floating with your very own mermaid tail. Your tail shimmers with many stunning colors and makes you feel light and lovely, but also powerful and energized, like you can do anything. This is incredible, and you feel so absolutely thrilled to be experiencing mermaid magic.

You swim out to your new mermaid friend, as you are now at one with the ocean. You swim so quickly with your lovely mermaid flipper tail gliding gracefully. Through the bubbling blue sea water, your new mermaid friend tells you her name, which is a secret. Now you are the only human being to know what her secret name is as you swim happily spinning and twirling through the ocean, hidden behind lots of tufts of soft green sea grass. Where the sea becomes deeper and deeper, she shows you the grand underwater palace made entirely of shells, and you explore the magnificent mermaid kingdom hidden in the Rainbow Reef in an exceptional spot.

Somewhere in the Great Barrier Reef, the gardens of the underwater, the palace is a coral garden. It is full of technicolor and magnificent. It is just stunning here with so many coral varieties, like the lettuce coral, brain coral and star corals in iridescent and magical colors. The happiest mermaid introduces you now to her mermaid friends, all very lovely and unique in their own ways and so happy to meet you. They show you some fun clownfish clowning around and making everyone laugh with their silly antics of parrotfish copying.

You burst out laughing. You love gazing into the rainbow fish shimmering beautifully with every color of the rainbow. Then there's the stonefish looking so stone-faced and serious for no reason at all with a puffed-up pout. You and your mermaid friends can't help but find it is hilariously funny. The mermaids show you how to play games with clams opening and closing to collect their sparkling pearls. You must be quick before they snap shut and giggle at you when you collect enough pearls. Your mermaid friends show you how to thread them onto a thin piece of green sea grass to make a gorgeous friendship bracelet of ocean pearls that fits perfectly around your dainty wrist.

The happiest mermaid loves nature and loves looking after her environment. That way, nature loves her and looks after her in the beautiful circle of life in the ocean. As you play, you notice the mermaids collecting spiky red crown-of-thorns starfish which are like litter on the reef. Because they eat the beautiful corals, the mermaids feed these red spikey starfish to the giant Triton seashells that munch them away like happy garbage collectors and keep the Barrier Reef clean and safe.

So, the corals can continue to grow and flourish, you patch the backs of these mighty Triton sea snails that do such important work to keep the reef healthy and magnificent. Suddenly, a pod of dolphins swims by and squeaks at you all. Now a race is on, as you swim and twirl and dive through the Rainbow Reef with the delighted dolphins. These shiny, smooth, pure and wise creatures lead you to the edge of the beautiful Great Barrier Reef. The happiest mermaid's eyes light up and she claps her hands with joy. Now you see the most majestic, peaceful, and massive creature of all moving through the deep ocean.

A blue whale. Wow! The huge blue whale drifts over to you and smiles with its cheeky little side grin and spurts a burst of air through its blowhole to say hello to you. You're amazed to be swimming with a whale, and such a funny, friendly whale. The happiest mermaid laughs at your disbelief as she shows you how to hold on to barnacles on the whale's back as you go for a whale ride, and you have a 'whale' of a time. The smooth skin of your blue whale friend glides with ease through the ocean depths. You feel so powerful and free and at one with all of nature and very happy after your unforgettable whale ride.

The happiest mermaid shimmies through the

reef back to the mermaid kingdom, and you swim with her as the sun now starts to set. It is evening now. It's time to make music together by blowing different shells that make unique sounds like horns and flutes and panpipes. One of the mermaids plays the drum by tapping the shell of an ancient turtle with some coral sticks. The baby clams join in as castanets, and the mermaids sing and dance to the natural rhythms. Your ocean band is so much fun as you love being part of this underwater community where everyone gets along so happily and easily.

You feel so safe and welcome and wonderful to be yourself because everybody loves you exactly as you are. As you swirl and swish about to the music, you realize that you love yourself exactly as you are, too. You feel so grateful for your divine life and all these fun and happy experiences. You get to enjoy just being you after having so much fun on the Rainbow Reef with the happiest mermaid and all of your new ocean creature friends. It is time now to return home for your healthy deep sleep.

The happiest mermaid whose name only you know swims with you to the white sands on the shore of your tropical island. As she gives you a happy giggle and a wave, your mermaid tail disappears in a sparkle of enchantment. You wave to your mermaid friend noticing you still have your pearl bracelet. You watch her dive and swim between the pure waves. As you float up above the tropical island and up above the beautiful blue ocean, you return home into your warm cozy bed as you sleep happily and dream blissfully.

You feel so loved and lucky to have swum with the mermaids, gone riding on a whale, looked after the reef environment, and to have had such fun wonderful ocean adventures.

My voice will leave you now as you dream happily and sleep deeply with total peace because you know that you can go on an enchanted mermaid journey to this secret Rainbow Reef anytime you wish. Sweet dreams.

Chapter 4
Funny Stories

MONKEYING AROUND

Once upon a time, in a jungle that was very, very far away from all the people, on an island that no human had ever stepped on, lived a family of monkeys. The monkeys lived in a very big group of monkeys, and they always had a great time playing with each other! They knew that they could always count on each other, and because of that, they always had fun doing things with each other. Sometimes, they would even play jokes on each other. They thought that their pranks on each other were very funny! But, sometimes, someone would do something that was not so nice after all. Sometimes, they would make someone sad with their pranks, and they would have to try to fix it before the other one is sad for too long.

So one day, the monkeys were talking. Two of them, named Molly and Missy, wanted to play a prank on the monkey named Mark. They thought that it would be very fun to joke with Mark because they knew that Mark would laugh! So, they spent a very long time trying to think of a really fun prank to play on him.

"Maybe we should jump out and pretend to be a lion?" said Molly.

"Nah," said Missy. "Maybe we should try to get a snake to catch him! That would get him!"

"No, that seems too mean," said Molly. "But... What if we made a vine that looked like a snake and used it to tie him up, so he thought it was real?"

Missy nodded. She liked that idea! So, they set off to come up with their snake that they were making. They decided that they would take a thick, green vine, and some thick mud to make a head on it. Then, they hid it on the ground, and they each took one end and hid on either side of a path that Mark would walk over. If Mark wanted to go and get any berries from the bush, he would have to walk right over the snake vine.

So, they waited and waited and waited some more. They waited so long for Mark to come along that they were both starting to get bored. They sighed, and they rolled around on the ground, and they almost missed Mark coming. But they heard him coming by, and they hid in the bushes. Mark walked over the snake, and they suddenly caught him with the vine! They wrapped it all around him and hid before he could see them.

Mark screamed and got very scared! He cried, "No, please, let go of me! HELP!"

And Missy and Molly started laughing very loudly in the bushes. They laughed, and they laughed, and they came out and picked up the vine. "It was a joke!" they said, still laughing.

Mark did not think the joke was very funny. He looked at them both sadly. Then, he looked at them both angrily. Then, he walked away without saying a word and without his berries.

"I don't think he thought it was funny," said Molly.

"I don't think so either," said Missy.

They both felt bad. The joke was supposed to be funny! The joke was supposed to be great! But they still both made him feel bad. "I think he was really scared," said Molly.

"Yeah..." said Missy, sadly.

They looked at each other. "We should do something for Mark to help him feel better."

"Yeah!" said Missy. "We should bring him some of the berries. Isn't that why he came here anyway?"

Molly nodded her head, and they picked up a great, big leaf. They filled up the leaf with all the best berries that they could find for Mark. "Maybe we should hide a spider in the berries..." said Molly.

"Molly!" said Missy. "No!" she shook her head. "I think we were already mean enough to Mark. Let's just give him his berries and leave him alone!"

"Yeah, you're right," said Molly. But she still really wanted to surprise Mark. She decided not to, though, because she thought that would be too mean.

When their berries were all picked up, they went to go find Mark. They looked at his tree, but he was not there. So, they went to go look somewhere else instead. They went to go try the river, but he was not there either. They looked all over the island with their berries, but they did not find him. The monkeys sat down to think. Where could he be?

But then, something scary happened. They heard a very loud roar, and something hit Molly in the back and knocked her over! It sounded like a tiger!

“No, stop!” they both cried. “Please don’t eat us!”

But then, they heard very loud laughing. They turned around and saw Mark sitting there. He had pretended to be a tiger to scare them, and it had worked!

“Mark!!” they both cried out, and then they started laughing.

They were both surprised, and then they realized that they knew how Mark felt when they had pretended to be a snake with the vine. “I’m sorry,” said Molly.”

“Me too, “said Missy. “We won’t scare you anymore.”

“But we got you some berries!” said Molly, and she held out the leaf that they had filled up. But the leaf had been crushed when they had tried to run! It was dripping with berry juice, all over the ground.

“Sorry...” they both said, laughing.

And both Molly and Missy learned something very important that day. They learned that there was no use in scaring others. They learned that there was no reason for them to be so hurtful toward others. But they also learned that they could be kind to their friends, too, and that was very important to them. So, they never played mean jokes again, and Molly, Missy and Mark were very good friends forever after.

At this point, our planet and every species need help. Climate change is now contributing to one of the two main causes for any species, plant or animal, becoming threatened, endangered or extinct. That cause is habitat destruction. While more people than ever are going green, which is wonderful and necessary, a large part of going green or being a conservationist is understanding why each and every species in our world is valuable, important and cannot be allowed to disappear. What every person who understands conservation (as well as millions of scientists over the world) knows is that every species in the natural world serves a purpose. Bees and other insects pollinate flowers that grow into fruit and vegetables. Ants clean the forest floor, which in turn leaves less opportunity for harmful bacteria to develop. The plant world supplies us with oxygen (the air that keeps us alive). As humans, we are part of the animal kingdom. As a part of the animal kingdom and life on earth, we must do our job to protect other plants and animals so that they can do their jobs, which benefit us in the long run. Similarly, it is our job to fix mistakes and heal wounds that we have caused to our natural world. Life depends on it.

Naima was a kind girl who loved being outside in nature. Naima loved everything about the natural world. Colors, light, the green grass, leaves in the trees - all those things gave Naima joy. Birds singing and flying above and animals that lived on the ground and the trees, all these things delighted her. Naima loved the fragrance of flowers and the call of different birds. All these things held the same value to Naima as her family. Her father had always taught her the importance of the natural world, and that if there was no natural world, there could be no people. While Naima loved nature as much as her father, she could not understand why there would be no humans if there were no natural world. She hoped that she would always be able to walk in her woods.

One day, Naima was in her sacred forest, hiking on her favorite trail. She looked around, admiring the flowers and the wind and every other part of being outside in nature. The air was warm and smelled like orchids and honeysuckle and the sea. Naima could not imagine a more beautiful fragrance. Then hmmm, hmmm, hmmm. Naima noticed that as she took a step, she heard a buzzing sound. "What is that?" she wondered. As she looked around, Naima could not see anything out of the ordinary. She kept walking. Bzz, bzz hmm, bzz. What is that? Naima wondered again. She stopped and looked around again. Then she heard a high squeak. Looking over to a hibiscus flower, she noticed a tiny bird.

"Well, hello there, little fellow," Naima said, smiling. "Aren't you adorable and beautiful?"

The little bird was genuinely magnificent, especially for something so tiny. As the sunlight shined on the small bird showing glittering colors like ruby red, emerald green and sapphire blue, Naima was dazzled. It was a hummingbird. Naima loved hummingbirds for their amazing colors and size. She thought they were the loveliest birds and often thought they were so perfect that they were more like something out of a dream.

"Thank you," the little bird said in a tiny voice. "And thank you for loving my home and wanting to keep it safe. That is very important because we are all connected."

"My Dad tells me that all the time," Naima said, smiling at the little bird. "Though I am not sure what that means." She liked the idea of being connected to all the beauty and life in the forest; she just did not know how she was. She wasn't related to birds or insects or bunnies. She knew that she was sort of related to monkeys, but that didn't mean that she was connected to them. At the same time though, Naima desperately wanted to be connected to all the life and beauty of the natural world. She thought that would be the best gift in the world.

"That is easy. Let me show you," said the little hummingbird. "Come with me."

As Naima followed the little bird, she looked

over and saw a bee at a flower. “Oh!” Naima said as she jumped out of the way. Naima didn’t want to be stung.

“That bee is one of the most important creatures in the world,” the hummingbird said.

“I love honey,” Naima said, smiling. She watched the little bee as it busily collected pollen from the flower.

“They don’t just make honey,” the hummingbird said. “Bees and other insects also help pollinate flowers, so that the flowers can reproduce. Remember how important plants are.”

“Yes, a lot of food comes from plants!” Naima said.

“If there were no bees, there would be a lot less food in the world, not to mention oxygen, which comes from plants and trees.”

“Wow, they do a lot for such little things!” Naima wondered who would pollinate all those plants and trees if there were no bees. Humans could not do that, there were not enough people to pollinate all those plants.

Suddenly Naima heard a loud squawk. Then a pair of parrots flew into a nearby tree.

“Yay! Parrots!” Naima cheered. Parrots were Naima’s most favorite birds after hummingbirds, of course.

“They are not just fun to look at, they are beneficial,” the hummingbird said. “Like most birds, they help trees by dropping fruits, nuts and seeds on the ground. Some of those seeds grow into new trees. Some are eaten by other animals that live on the ground and some fertilize the soil.”

“Wow! That is amazing! Birds do a lot,” Naima said. “The trees that grow from those seeds bear fruit, which feeds other animals, including me! Without those trees, there would not be as much food for any of us. And let’s not forget that trees and other plants produce oxygen. All life on earth needs oxygen to breathe! We all need both of those things to survive.”

“That’s right!” the hummingbird chirped. “Now, see all those leaves falling?”

Looking over where the hummingbird told her, Naima did see leaves falling to the ground. She noticed that the branches from where the leaves were falling were moving.

“Monkeys? Squirrels? What is it?” Naima asked excitedly. She wanted to learn more about how vital her favorite things were.

"I think those are monkeys," the hummingbird said. "But it could be squirrels. Both of them knock leaves and fruits to the ground. Those fruits are sometimes eaten by other animals who distribute the seeds. They do that by eating the fruits and moving and jumping on the branches. This causes the fruit and leaves to fall to the ground. Some of the fruit is eaten by creatures that live on the ground. The fruits and leaves that are not eaten decompose and fertilize the soil so that it can nourish more trees and plants."

Naima looked at the ground and noticed that it too was teeming with life. She saw ants carrying leaves on their backs. "Look at that!" Naima said, pointing at the hardworking little insects.

"I told you, bees are not the only useful members of the insect world," the hummingbird chirped. "Those ants work hard to clean up the forest floor. Other insects till the soil so that plants can grow. Even worms help! Worms aerate the soil so that more oxygen and water can get to the roots of the plants and trees, bringing them nutrients to help them grow."

"That is just amazing!" Naima cheered. "Who knew how important worms and ants could be!"

As Naima and her tiny bird friend moved along, they came upon a crystal-clear creek. Naima loved the sound of water almost as much as she loved birdsong. As she leaned over to drink from the water, Naima noticed tiny fish swimming by.

“Oh, look!” Naima said. “Aren’t they adorable!”

“The animals in the water are just as important!” the hummingbird continued. “In both fresh and saltwater, everyone does their part to keep the world clean and healthy for us all.”

“What do they do?” Naima asked if she loved snorkeling and surfing. “I love swimming and being in the water. There is so much beauty in the water. But how do sea creatures help us?”

“Well, some of the creatures that live in water keep it clean so that it doesn’t get polluted. They swim close to the bottom and eat food particles, which makes their seafloor home clean. The seaweeds also help to keep the waters clean; they catch pollution and silt, preventing them from floating all over and poisoning the underwater world. Aquatic plants also help produce oxygen. Some animals eat seagrass, helping it spread elsewhere. Some keep other sea animals from overpopulating. And let us not forget animals like beavers. By building their dams, those busy little rodents build homes that act as filters which prevent anything dangerous from traveling into larger bodies of water.”

"Wow! That is so fascinating. Beavers clean the water with their dams, seagrass keeps the oceans clean. Even predators are useful, because if there were too many animals living in the ocean or a lake, or even on land, they would cause more pollution, and there would only be mud. Where would we get fresh water to drink?" Naima was amazed. "We are all connected!"

Naima smiled at all she had learned that day from her tiny hummingbird friend. It was a fact that they were all connected. In nature, Naima realized that everything needs everything else. And that included humans. Without plants, water, and other creatures, there would be no humans.

"This is all so amazing. And now I can explain to others why it is so important to protect our world and all of its inhabitants!" Naima said. "I can teach everyone how we are all connected and how everything, plants, animals and even insects help to keep the world sustainable and healthy for all of us. That means that we need each other. No matter the species or even life form. Everything is important. We all exist thanks to everything else!"

"And they will listen to you because you will be presenting facts rather than just your opinion," the little hummingbird said. "Although I certainly think that your opinion is valid and I love it."

“And I love you!” Naima said. “I love all of you, and we will always be connected. I can’t thank you enough.”

“Spread the word, which will be all the thanks we need!” the hummingbird said. Then off the tiny bird flew.

That night, Naima dreamed of flying with the birds in the sky and swimming underwater on a reef teaming with life. She also dreamed that she was a garden surrounded by hundreds of flowers and hummingbirds. That was her favorite dream ever.

Sweet dreams little one.

THE DEER AND THE BEAR

This story tells the tale of animals who learned that, despite their differences, they all still deserved to be treated fairly and equally. It revolves around a young deer who was always told by her mother that everyone was equal. This story teaches problem-solving and dealing with others.

Once, a long time ago, when animals roamed the earth and humans were not around, there was an animal named Meg. Meg was a deer, she walked on four legs, her body was covered in fur and she had a bushy white tail. She was very quick and could hop around the forest on her four legs. She spent most of her time by the forest lake with other plant-eaters like her. One of her friends was Murry the moose. She was also friends with Ella the elk and Donnie, another deer like her, except he was a boy deer and had antlers. These animals loved eating plants, drinking water and playing by the banks. That is until some new animals appeared.

It was common knowledge that if the new animals, the meat-eaters, came in, the plant-eating animals would have to leave. Meg was a young deer and didn't understand that this was the way of life for all the animals that ate plants. Her mother had always told her that everyone was equally important. If the plant-eaters must move out of the way for the animals that ate meat, then it didn't sound to Meg like they were all equal. She decided to ask some of the other animals why this was. After all, it sounded like they were not equal to her. Meg headed over deeper into the forest to speak to other animals and see what they had to say. They must know because she thought that the animals that lived deeper in the woods were older and many of them were different from her.

"I don't get it, why do we always have to run away whenever those who eat meat appear?" Meg asked old Gus and Ajax, the beavers who were busy building a dam in the busy river.

"Well," Gus began. "It's just how it is." Then Gus put his head underwater to grab some mud from the bottom.

"It's always been that way," Ajax explained, "As soon as someone sees that the meat-eaters are coming, we have to hide." He busied himself patting on the dam to make sure it was secure.

"Or else we might get eaten, " Gus continued as he joined Ajax in building the dam, "Nobody wants to be dinner, you see, Little Meg."

"Well, I certainly do not want to be dinner," Meg said. "But it doesn't seem right. It isn't fair!"

"No, it doesn't," Old Ajax agreed, his mouth full of twigs. "And no, it is not fair either."

"It's just the way it is," Gus said, and the old beavers continued building.

Meg moved on to a field where some other older deer were lying about and enjoying the sun.

"Hi guys," Meg said as she greeted them.

"Hi, dear Meg," said her uncle Barney. "What can we do for you today?" Uncle Barney was lying in clover and eating bits of clover as he lay in the sun soaking up the warmth.

"I was wondering why we always have to move when the meat-eaters show up. My mom said that everyone is equal, are we not equal to them?"

"Well, you see," Byron, a buck with the biggest antlers in the field said, "It's simple, really. None of us want to get eaten."

"I don't get it, what makes them so important?" Meg asked. "What gives them the right to eat us?"

"Well, they are bigger and stronger than we are," Byron explained. "It's just the way it is."

"They are smaller than a moose!" Megs argued, "Moose are the largest of all of us!"

"Well," Barney said, "While that is true, the meat-eaters can move very fast and are more aggressive."

Meg thought about this for a moment.

“What if we made friends with them to show them that we are just as good as they are?” Meg asked.

“That won’t happen,” Barney continued. “They are bigger and stronger and fiercer than we are, and it is just better that we stay out of their way.”

This was going nowhere, so Meg decided it was time to move on.

As Meg moved along, she hoped she would find some plant-eaters that had more courage.

Soon she found Steve the ram grazing with some of his friends.

“I have a question,” Meg began. “Why are we less important than the meat-eaters?”

“I don’t think we are,” said Ollie the ram. “But they always push everyone else around.”

“But there are more of us than there are of them,” Meg said.” What if we stood up to them?”

“That might not work,” Steve said. “Everyone is afraid of getting eaten.”

“What if we made friends with them, then they might not eat us,” suggested Meg again, hoping for a better response. And she got one.

"It's worth a try," Steve said. "But don't get your hopes up because it's never been that way before."

"We'll go with you," Ollie said. "We'll help to try to make friends with them, and we will protect you if it doesn't work."

"Thanks!" said Meg hoping that it would work. And off the three friends went.

Soon they found a young bear. Even though the bear was young, he was gigantic. He was just standing around roaring. It was loud enough to give anyone a headache. The three friends were just about to run away when Meg noticed a tear dripping down the bear's face. He was crying. Why, he is just a big baby, thought Meg. She walked toward the big crying bear cub.

"Be careful!" Ollie and Steve warned. "Even though he is a baby, he is still a bear."

"Are you alright?" asked Meg carefully approaching the crying giant.

"No!" sobbed the bear. "I'm lost, and I can't find my mommy! I keep calling her, but she isn't here, and I'm so frightened I don't know what to do!" And then the bear cub continued to sob and wale so loudly that Meg was sure that he could be heard all over the world!

“We’ll help you,” said Meg. “We can find your mother, and we will make sure that you are safe.”

“We will?” Ollie asked, surprised that anything that large had a mommy.

“We can?” Steve asked. He was not so sure that they should help a gigantic baby find his even more gigantic meat-eating mother.

“Yes, we can, and yes, we will,” Meg said. “If we want everyone to be equal, we have to show that we are. If we want kindness from meat-eaters like his mother, we have to show them kindness.”

“I don’t know,” said Steve. “I am in favor of a kind act, but this is a bear we are talking about.” He was worried about how a mother bear would feel about three plant-eaters escorting her baby. “What if she thinks we are trying to harm the big baby?”

“We have to try,” said Meg. Then she turned to the weeping bear, “My name is Meg.”

“I’m Ron,” he sniveled.

“I am pleased to meet you, Ron,” Meg said, smiling. “This is Steve and Ollie, and we are going to get you back to your mother."

The four new friends took no time to find Ron's mother, who was so happy to see Ron safe that she proceeded to give the biggest bear hug in the world to Meg, Steve and Ollie, as well as Ron.

"Momma!" Ron roared happily.

"Thank you so much for bringing my little baby back to me!" Momma said to Meg, Steve and Ollie, who were all sure that there was nothing little about the baby.

"You are welcome," Meg said.

"I don't mean to be rude, because I am so grateful that you found him," Momma said. "But why did you help him? I know that your kind and mine never get along."

"We want to change that," Meg said. "I believe that we are all equal and that nobody is more important than anyone else, and we all deserve the same rights and privileges. I wanted to see if we could make friends with someone like you so that your kind might not chase us away or eat us."

"Well, now you have two new friends," Momma said, "and we will make sure that you have many friends with us meat-eaters. Besides, we're bears, we usually eat fish"

The next day, Ron and Momma appeared at the big river. The beavers started to go underwater. The rams prepared to strike with their horns. The bucks lowered their antlered heads, ready to charge. Meg ran over to her new friends with Steve and Ollie.

"No! Stay! These are our friends!" Meg called out to the others. "There is no need to be afraid!"

"They are going to eat us!" yelled a rabbit.

"No! They are here to visit us and talk!" Meg said. "They are our new friends!"

"They want to tell us that we all belong too!" Steve called out.

"Remember, we are all equal!" Ollie said. "We have to show our acceptance of them, and they will accept us as equal to them!"

"You are my friends," Ron said.

"We never eat friends!" Momma said. "I promise, from now on, our kind will treat your kind as equals and friends. We only want to celebrate our friendship with a drink from the lake."

Soon the plant-eaters began to approach Ron

and Momma to shake hands.

And so, the entire group moved to the river, and each took a long drink. Then they played and splashed in the water for hours afterward. By the end of the day, every animal was covered in mud and ready for a good night's sleep. And they were also all friends.

True to her word, Momma made sure that her new friends would be accepted and treated with kindness and equality by all the other meat-eaters, instead of bullying and eating them. And from then on, whenever meat-eaters approached the lake or the river, the plant-eaters did not run away in fear. Instead, they all lived together peacefully. Ron and Meg played all day every day. And at the end of each day, they curled up together and fell asleep counting the stars. They dreamed of adventures in the sky, water and forests.

Sweet dreams little one.

THE GOOD BEARS

Loving others despite their differences is a difficult lesson to learn. This story tells the tale of a young gopher named Bonnie and how she learned to love others when some giant bears came to her town. This story is a great way to get children to understand diversity and unity with people of all nations who live in their neighborhood. You can use this story to begin to talk about some of the prejudice that we have about other people based on not knowing anything about them.

There was once a little village on the prairie called Yesterville. Every building in Yesterville was made of wood and thatched little roofs. All the buildings looked the same, except for that of old Annie's house, which seemed to be falling apart. There were many creatures in that land when the gophers moved in and built the village, but no one knew where they came from. The forest creatures stayed away from the prairie village because it was populated mostly by gophers, and they didn't seem to want to bother them. Many of the prairie dogs that lived in the area before moved away for the same reason.

The gophers of the village did not interact much with the town that the prairie dogs lived in and stayed away from many of the other towns if they could. They did not like their children to interact with outsiders. The gophers of Yesterville did not even talk much to the prairie dogs that stayed in the village, because they thought of them as wild. The only time anyone ever left the village was to go out hunting, which was a sport that they loved. In the village, there was a bakery and a market, a church and a school. Everyone in the village would dress in the same manner and would even believe the same things. Overall, they were very content with the life that they had and had moved away from their homeland because it was filled with all different types of animals and they wanted to remain separate.

The inhabitants of the village of Yesterville didn't know that the town was built right in the middle of bear country. This is usually not a problem because bears are generally kind and generous. They would always help people who needed help. The bears were also nomadic, meaning that they moved around from place to place with the changing of the seasons. The people who had lived there for a long time knew that the bears would come every summer. And in the before times, people would leave out treats for the bears, such as fish and honey and all kinds of delicious goodies to thank them for all the kind acts that they had done for them over the years. Some of the kind acts that the Bears did during those before times were that they fixed homes and other buildings that had been damaged or ruined during the winter. Winter was always a very hard time in Yesterville.

Often during the before times, the bears would bring the people fruits and vegetables from the south; the people who lived in the prairie had often been very appreciative of the generosity of the bears and grateful for those fruits that hadn't grown there in the past. The bears would also make sure that, before they left, the people would have enough firewood to get them comfortably through the long winter months. All the animals in the area loved the bears because they would give them food to eat, and the wild animals did not fear the bears because the bears were very kind.

Of course, since the Yesterville gophers didn't want to mix with the prairie dogs of the area or the animals from other villages, or the wild animals of the woods, they didn't know anything about the bears that would come. So it was a surprise when they heard the ground rumble with the coming of the bears. There were so many bears that the sound of them marching back to the prairie lands sounded like a stampede. The people of Yesterville were very scared and ran outside to see what was happening. Then they ran back inside because they were scared of the bears. They had never seen so many bears at one time before, and bears are very big, especially compared to a gopher.

There was one little girl named Bonnie, who watched the bears as they approached the village. She had never seen such a large animal before. She got afraid because her parents were afraid. Everyone in the village who was not a bear, which was everyone, was afraid of the bears. Bonnie looked out the window and watched as the bears spoke to each other and pointed at the little village. The bears seemed confused; it hadn't been there last spring. Then one of the bears looked at the sign for the village. They started talking to each other and were studying the village sign. They were such large animals and yet they spoke very quietly. Bonnie found them to be odd, but not as scary as everyone else seemed to think they were. There was one bear who then decided to say something.

The bear cupped his hands around his mouth and yelled out, "Hello, Yesterville," he had an accent that made him hard to understand, but if you listened carefully, it was easy to tell what he was saying.

Bonnie was shocked at how loud a bear could yell, and she watched out the window to see if anyone would come out of their homes to greet the bears. Everyone stayed in their houses; they were way too afraid.

"Hello, Yesterville," the giant bear said again. Then he pointed to himself and said, "Ben."

All of the villagers of Yesterville stayed in their homes.

Bonnie kept watching the giant bears; she had

never seen animals like them before. She thought that not only were they large, but they looked sort of like really big gophers, only a little different. Most of the bears were brown, but some of them were black and others had tan fur. The men had big beards and the women wore long braids in their hair. Their arms and legs reminded Bonnie of tree trunks. Bonnie had never seen anyone that didn't look like her family, except for the wildwood animals that were nearly afraid to come into the town. She was born in Yesterville and never really interacted with people that were not like her. Everyone in Yesterville was a gopher like her.

"What savage creatures," said Bonnie's mother. "Let's get away from the windows."

Bonnie listened to her mother's directions and moved away from the window.

"Why are they savages, Momma?" asked Bonnie.

"Because we are civilized, we wear proper clothes and live in this village."

"Oh, right," said Bonnie. Bonnie thought she must be silly for thinking the bears were just like her. Although, she didn't know that they were bears yet.

"Are they just really big gophers, momma?"

"No, they are not like us at all, they are bears."

"Why are bears savages, momma?" asked Bonnie.

"Savages are people that are not like us," said her mother.

Bonnie began thinking about what it would be like to meet one of the savage bears.

"Besides," added her mother, "Bears will eat us."

Outside a bear was yelling "Hello" over and over again.

"Oh, dear!" Bonnie said, horrified. That sounded awful.

After about an hour the bears shrugged their shoulders and walked away; they probably went to another town to see what was wrong with Yesterville. The gophers of Yesterville stayed in their homes all day and all night. Bonnie was told to go to bed early, but she couldn't sleep. She kept thinking about the giant bears and how they looked pretty much like really big gophers. Bonnie worried that the bears might come back and eat her neighbors for dinner.

Bonnie finally began to think that the bears were huge and ugly and savage just like her mother had said. She thought about how her parents knew so much and wondered how they knew so much. She wondered how they knew that bears would eat them for dinner.

The next day, Bonnie woke up and got dressed. She went to the window to look and see if the giant savage bears were outside, but the bears were not there. Looking outside she noticed that no one was walking around outside either. Her mother told her that school would be canceled for the day because everyone was going to stay inside in case the bears came back.

Bonnie tried to entertain herself in the house all morning, but she felt so very bored. Eventually, she decided to go outside. Since no one was outside, she would have the whole world to herself. However, Bonnie couldn't stop thinking about the bears. She began having a feeling she had never had before; she was curious about the bears. She walked along the roads of the town and noticed that her friend Anne's house looked brand new. She thought that was weird because Anne's house had been damaged in a storm during the long winter, and it seemed like it would have taken a whole year to fix. She also noticed that someone had planted a beautiful garden in front of the house, all since the last time she had been there. She wondered how that happened. Everything looked beautiful, and Bonnie wondered who had fixed Anne's home overnight.

Bonnie decided to try and find the giant bears. She just wanted to look at them and maybe see if they were eating any gophers. She had never felt this curious about anything or anyone before. While she knew that her mother would be angry with her for leaving Yesterville, since it had long been a tradition that the children were not allowed to go past the town's borders, she didn't care much. She was a little concerned that her father would be very mad with her and punish her when she came back, but she just felt that it was her destiny to see those giant bears again. They might be savages, but she didn't think they would have spent so much time trying to say hello if they were mean.

It didn't take her very long to find the tribe of bears. She hid behind a big tree and hoped that no one would see her. The giant bears were sitting in a circle around a big campfire; they were eating honey and fish and laughing. One bear began to play an enormous instrument and they all began to sing. It was the loveliest music that Bonnie had ever heard, and it made her smile. She could not remember when in her life she had heard such beautiful music before, and it made Bonnie want to dance.

Bonnie began to tap her feet and then the next thing she knew she was swaying back and forth.

Suddenly, she felt a hand on her shoulder. It was a very small bear that was probably a baby bear. She was very scared at that moment.

"Hello. Would you like to join us?" the bear asked in a surprisingly gentle voice.

"Pu, Pu, please don't eat me," was all that Bonnie could say.

"Eat you?" asked the bear gently, "Why would we do that?"

"Don't bears eat gophers?"

"No!" the bear laughed. "We only eat fish for meat! Where on earth did you get that idea?"

"My mother said that you are savages," Bonnie said, feeling rather silly. "And that savages eat gophers."

"I thought savages moved onto other people's land and then ignore them," the bear said.

"We've never seen a bear before," Bonnie said, "I don't think any of us knew this was your land. Besides, my momma thought you were going to eat us, so it's quite understandable that we were afraid."

"We figured that," the bear said, "So my poppa and my uncle fixed one of the broken homes and we left"

"You fixed Anne's house?"

"Yeah, that's what we bears do, we help people who need help," the bear said. "It's our way of life."

Bonnie had never heard of strangers helping people, but she liked the idea.

"Are you hungry?" the bear asked.

"I am," said Bonnie.

"Well, come along, there is plenty for everyone, we even have some fruits and veggies from down south of here, we were going to give them to the people of your town, but no one would come out. You can meet my dad; his name is Ben. My name is Zack."

"I'm Bonnie"

Bonnie thought the giant bears were lovely company, and they seemed to know everything about the whole wide world. She had never seen so many bears and other animals hanging around a campfire before; they seemed to be friends with everyone. Ben told her that, because the bears would help injured animals when they needed help, everyone loved them. She had three helpings of the giant bear's dinner because it was so delicious.

"I love it here," said Bonnie.

"Thank you," said Zack. "We always have fun around the campfire. And you are welcome to come play with us whenever you want."

Ben, Zack and a few of the other bears helped Bonnie get back home. As she and the giant bears came back to Yesterville, she noticed that many of the gophers of the town had gathered and had formed a hunting party.

"Don't eat her," yelled Bonnie's mother.

"No, momma, I am fine," Bonnie said as she ran over to her mother. "I went for a walk and found Ben and the other giants. They fed me and brought me home. And they fixed Anne's house and planted that beautiful garden for her."

"What?" Bonnie's mom and dad asked.

"They aren't like us," said Bonnie, "and they aren't savages. They are kind bears and they help people wherever they go. They are good animals, and they are my newest friends."

"How?" asked Bonnie's mother.

"Just because they're different from us, Momma, doesn't make them scary," said Bonnie. "They are kind and generous. We were just afraid because we didn't know anything about them. But here is the thing, just because someone is different doesn't make them bad. I think they are nicer than people in our town because they helped fix Anne's house and didn't ask for anything in return, they just did it because it was the right thing to do. Besides, it's needed help for so long and no one in the town would help fix it."

This made all the gophers of Yesterville stop and think about if what she said was true. It was true that no one had helped Anne and her family fix the house until the giant bears came.

"You're right, Bonnie," said her father, "you saw them with a better heart than we did."

Then he hugged her and said to Ben, "Would you like to join us for some dessert?"

"We certainly would enjoy that, I'm so hungry I could eat a gopher!" Ben joked. "Just kidding, we don't eat gophers, the only meat we eat is fish. Besides, bears love eating sweets."

From that day on the gophers of Yesterville

loved the giant bears and did nothing but show them kindness and friendship. Zack and Bonnie met all the other kids, and eventually, all the kids were allowed to leave the town to play in the wild with the gentle bears. The people began to include the bears in all their celebrations and social events, and even built a hall big enough to let the bears in too. The gophers of Yesterville had learned not to judge thanks to the giants. They changed the name of their town to "Welcomeville" to let everyone know that they were welcome. They began to become friends with all the different animals in the area, especially the prairie dogs. Bonnie liked the way life was after meeting the bears; everyone in the village became more curious and interested in learning more and loving people more. Bonnie knew that she had the bears to thank for this.

Sweet Dreams, little one.

THE LITTLE MERMAID

Once upon a time, deep in the ocean, a little mermaid named Mariana lived. Mariana had a long, lavender-colored tail with the most beautiful fins, and her long, silver hair would float around her like curtains as she swam. She was the princess of the merpeople, and she lived with her father, her several siblings and her grandmother in a great underwater castle.

Mermaids were not allowed to swim up to the surface—it was expressly forbidden. They were not allowed to see the sky until they turned 15 years old. Mariana's birthday was very, very soon. She was very excited, for she heard that there was nothing as beautiful as the sky or the grass. She had heard lots of stories from her older siblings who told her that the world above the sea was great, but under the sea was so much better. Still, Mariana wanted to see the shore. She wanted to see the strange people called Humans who walked around on two feet. She wanted to know what they knew. She wanted to see what they saw. And above all else, she wanted to know the feeling of sunlight on her face.

On Mariana's birthday, she was thrilled! She brushed out her hair. She polished her scales to make sure that they were perfectly shiny. She swam excitedly to her father. "Father, Father!" she said happily with a big grin on her face.

Mariana's father, the sea king, smiled at her. He was very fond of his youngest daughter, and he knew that she would be very eager to get out and see the world. Still, he was worried that something would happen to his dearest daughter. He was worried that she would do something and get into trouble, and there would be nothing that he could do about it. He looked at his daughter fondly. “What is it, Mariana?” he asked.

“I’m ready to go!” she said.

“Already? We haven’t even had breakfast yet!” said the sea king, pointing to the table full of food that was being brought out by mermaids who worked in the castle.

“I’m not hungry. I’ll be back soon!” she said quickly and with that, she was off before her father could say a word in objection.

So, off Mariana went. She swam up to the top of the water. With every stroke of her tail through the water, she got closer and closer to the surface. She could see the water getting brighter and brighter, and her eyes were very wide. She never realized how deep the water was!

She made it to the surface and swam up quickly. She could not breathe out of the water, for her body was meant to breathe underneath, but it was very, very beautiful. She could feel the warm sun on her face and her hair. She could feel the breeze, strange and chilling, but pleasant. She could see nothing but blue for miles and miles around her.

She did not know where she was, but she knew one thing was for sure— everywhere she looked, it was a beautiful sight to see!

Every few seconds, Mariana had to go underwater to take a breath, but she did so happily. She was thrilled to get to see this strange, new world, and though it was foreign, the sights of clouds floating through the sky like whales swimming past her in the ocean was absurd enough to make her laugh. She thought that the whole world was very, very silly!

Mariana felt like she could stay there for hours! She knew that it was very, very pretty and she was very desperate to stay there for a very long time. She knew that, ultimately, she wanted to be able to see the world before she swam home. She wanted to see the sunset and the strange two-legged Humans!

Soon, however, the sky began to get cloudy. There was water falling from it and the waves got big. She saw a big wooden boat in the distance and then heard yelling. She swam underwater as fast as she could to see what had happened.

She found a Human under the water! She swam to the Human to get him and pull him out. She was very worried for him, as she knew that these humans breathed air, not water as she did. She pulled him out of the water and onto the shore.

He was very, very beautiful, but she did not think that she would get to talk to him. So she sang him the most beautiful song that she could while she waited for someone else to find him, or for him to wake up.

Eventually, he started to wake up as there was shouting on the beach. Mariana saw the other people coming, so she swam all the way home.

But, Mariana could not stop thinking about the man, for she was in love with him. She knew that she wanted to love him as long as she could, but there was no way for her to go on shore with him! She had no feet.

As Mariana swam sadly home, she was stopped by a sea witch. "What's wrong, dear?" said the witch.

"I'm very sad, for I have met a prince that I love, but I cannot be with him!" said Mariana.

"I can help you with that," said the sea witch, and Mariana was very happy to take any help she could get. The deal was that Mariana would give the sea witch her beautiful voice, and in exchange, Mariana could go to the shore with her legs. But, if she could not get the beautiful man to fall in love with her within three days, she would lose her voice forever.

So, off Mariana went, and she swam up to the surface of the ocean. Once she got there and her face touched the air, she felt her body changing! Her fin became feet, and she had to swim all the way to shore without her tail.

When she got to the shore, she saw the man looking around, confused. She opened her mouth to talk to him, but nothing came out. She was very quiet and her voice was gone!

The man walked up to her. “What are you doing in the ocean?” he asked her, but she could only shake her head no because she could not talk.

So, the man took her home, telling her about how he was a prince and that he had been washed up to shore, but he could have sworn that a very beautiful woman with the most beautiful voice had saved him. He told her that he wanted to find that woman and fall in love with her forever after, but he could not figure out how to hunt her down.

Mariana very badly wanted to tell him that it was her, but she could not. So, off they went, and in the next two days, they became very good friends. But on day three, Mariana saw something terrible! She saw the sea witch with human legs, using her voice to sing to the prince! She was convincing him that she had saved him—and he believed it!

Mariana was shocked! She had been the one to save the prince! And then she saw it—a seashell around the witch's neck. That had to be where her voice was stored! So, Mariana only had one choice—she had to take back that seashell and get her voice back.

Off she went to figure out how to get it. She tried very hard, but the witch was not going to give it to her. Mariana was very sad then. She thought that she would have to live without her voice forever! She began to cry, but there were no sounds at all.

At the royal wedding, Mariana watched sadly, but there was nothing she could do.

But then, something amazing happened! A bird came down and stole away the seashell! It thought that the shell was food! When it realized that the seashell had no food, it dropped the necklace and the necklace broke. Once it broke, out came all of the magic that was there to stop her from singing. The spell was broken!

So Mariana began to sing at the back of the ship. The prince realized what had happened and the sea witch, without her magical seashell, turned back into her true form. She fell into the water and swam away, very embarrassed.

And the prince went to Mariana. "It was you!"

he said in awe of her singing. “You saved me!”

Mariana told him everything. She told him that she was a mermaid and that she was trying to become human because she loved him so much. He was very touched by her declaration and he decided that he would marry her. So, they went off to get married and they lived happily ever after.

Conclusion

By finishing this book, you get an overview of several animals and oceanic creatures and their potential in making the world a better place. You have discovered life underwater, including that of the mermaids, how the angelfish became a hero, barracuda's discovery and other stories.

These stories are unique to Bedtime Meditation Stories for Kids and will have an incredible impact on helping them sleep, while also helping them learn life lessons.

Remember that the grounding and meditation exercises that have been given in this book can be useful for both you and your children. The physical and mental benefits of meditation are very real and can improve the quality of life for children and adults alike. As you and your child get into this book, feel free to mix and match the exercises to tailor the book for you both. You know your child best. We want you to get the best possible result as you can from this book, so use it however you think is best!

We have covered several stories in the book to help you and your child relax with a series of meditation content. The stories will also enable your children to become critical thinkers as they evaluate and understand the moral of the stories. This book can be a very powerful tool to promote understanding of different life lessons and how to become heroes.

If you haven't done the meditations in this book with your child or implemented the tips and techniques that are described herein, your next step should be to do so! Working with your child to nail down a nightly routine that is as nourishing for your child as it is for you will help you to maintain the harmony you work for so hard to achieve in your home and with your family.

You can share these stories with your child time and time again. Each time they are read, something new will appear to your child. It will reinforce the importance of courage, friendship, gratefulness and family. Make sure you enjoy the time you spend with your child when reading these stories. Make it a fun and enjoyable way to end the day.

As a result of regular meditation, your child should notice positive results during the day as well. They might find that, by taking a break from thinking about certain a issue or problem, they were better able to come back to it with a fresh set of eyes, so to speak, and to unravel the issue they had been having.

This can give your child the tools to deal with life and the whatever waits in the day ahead. Having a good night's sleep makes all the difference, and you can make all the difference in whether or not that happens for them consistently.

The more we talk about our emotions and feelings, the closer those conversations bring us as a family. I hope that the stories in this book have led to many great conversations and discussions between you and your child, and that they will lead to more in the future.

It has been a pleasure spending time with you and your child, helping to encourage growth and mindfulness in relationships, and simply entertaining you with stories. Thank you for purchasing my book and for reading it. I hope you go back and reread the stories again and again and that they become some of your favorites on your bookshelf.

Printed in Great Britain
by Amazon

56479408R00133